WIRED SECRET

PARADISE CRIME THRILLERS BOOK 7

TOBY NEAL

"A woman's heart is a deep ocean of secrets."
~*Gloria Stuart*

CHAPTER ONE

SOMETIMES JUSTICE WASN'T FAIR.

Security specialist Sophie Ang stared with dislike at the twitchy blonde woman on the bed in the jail's infirmary. Holly Rayme's gaunt face was blotchy with the green and yellow of fading bruising.

"I am in hell." Rayme picked at a scab on the back of her hand as she addressed Sophie, Detective Kamani Freitan, and Hazel Matsue, a U.S. Marshal brought in to interview her for inclusion in the national Witness Protection Program. "You have to get me out of here."

"Things could actually be a lot worse." Freitan said. The tall, voluptuous mixed Hawaiian woman exuded volatility. Ancient Hawaiian chieftesses had accompanied their men into battle, and in another age, Freitan would have been perfectly in character carrying a club ringed with sharks' teeth instead of the police issue Glock she currently wore. "You've been hiding out in a soft bed in the infirmary. Got your own TV, even."

"I had to go through detox this week in this supposed comfy bed with my own TV. You think that wasn't hell?"

"You drug, you lose. And it would have been a lot worse out in gen pop. You've had protection outside your door 24/7. But if that

1

protection is going to continue, we need to know we have your full cooperation."

Rayme's watery blue eyes blinked. "You don't give a shit about me. I get that, loud and clear."

"You made your living robbing and extorting people. And now you're going to get out of jail," Freitan said. "I don't have to like that. Or you."

"We know you've been through a hard time, Holly." Sophie stepped forward to try to defuse the tension as Matsue looked on, arms folded. "But you had medical support, and you're through the worst of detox. You're fortunate. Ms. Matsue here is willing to take you into protective custody, provide you with a new identity, and relocate you until you can testify."

"Yes. I'm here to interview you, do your intake, and explain the program." Matsue was a slender woman with a triangular face. Though she wore black pants, a white shirt and a shiny gold Marshal's badge, Matsue had an innate style that set her apart, conveyed by deep red lipstick and an angular, asymmetrical bobbed haircut. She would have looked completely at home in Paris or Madrid rather than in the dingy jail infirmary with its bloom of ceiling mold and lingering smell of Lysol. "Do you understand why you've been referred to the Witness Protection Program, Ms. Rayme? And that you must comply with our procedures and directives? The U.S. Marshals Service has a one hundred percent success rate in protecting its clients if they follow WITSEC directions and protocols."

"All this 'special treatment' is because I'll be testifying against the Changs and helping you bring down a crime family. But I don't see that I have much choice," Rayme grumbled. "I know I'm lucky to be alive. My boyfriend Jimmy isn't."

Jim Webb and Holly Rayme had been involved in an investigation Sophie had just completed that had resulted in the apprehension of the Chang family's sadistic enforcer, Akane Chang. Holly's boyfriend had not survived an assassination attempt in the general population of the jail once the couple's importance as witnesses became evident, and Holly had barely survived her own attack.

"Can I turn this prisoner over to your custody?" Freitan asked Matsue. "I've got work to do."

"I have some paperwork for Ms. Rayme to fill out and forms for you to sign." Matsue handed paperwork on a clipboard to Rayme. "Once it's done, we can process her out of here." Matsue turned to address Sophie. "You've been a part of this team since I got here, but I'm unclear on your role, Ms. Ang."

"I work for a private firm, Security Solutions." Sophie's ongoing attachment to the case had been a new development. She and her partner Jake Dunn had wrapped up their contract to find a missing girl, and she'd tried to resume the vacation and hiking trip for which she'd come to the Big Island. Only days later, she'd been contacted by her employer to assist in security and support for Holly Rayme. "The families of Akane Chang's victims contracted with Security Solutions to pay for my services to support regular law enforcement."

"The U.S. Marshals Service does not work with private entities," Matsue said frostily.

"You want to work with this chick," Freitan said. "She's former FBI and a computer wizardess. Can't hurt to have her in your back pocket."

"And she's a badass bitch with a mean left hook," Rayme volunteered. "I happen to know. She and her partner were the ones to find out our part in the hustle we did with Akane Chang. And the only reason I'm saying anything nice is because her partner adopted our dog, and she can help keep me alive."

Endorsement by these two unlikely allies almost made Sophie smile. "I am on retainer, and available to help and support you," she told Matsue. "If you choose not to work with me, I will help from the sidelines. We should at least talk so I can explain how my skill set might be of use to you." Sophie held Matsue's skeptical gaze.

"Well, if that's all, I've got perps to bust and the day's a-wasting," Freitan said. "See you ladies at the trial." She turned and headed for the door.

As Freitan's hand touched the knob, an alarm ululated outside. The dome light out in the hallway began spinning, throwing red beams across Freitan. The muffled crack of a gunshot sounded out in the hall.

"Shit!" Freitan drew her weapon and flattened herself against the doorjamb, reaching over to turn the heavy silver bolt that locked the door. "We need to stay in here and guard the prisoner."

"Lower the blind over the window, Detective!" Matsue barked. "Ms. Rayme, get down off the bed and behind some cover!"

Sophie, as a civilian, had surrendered her Glock upon entering the jail. She felt its loss keenly as she helped Rayme, groaning and exclaiming, down off the bed. "I've had experience with an attack in a room like this. This equipment makes good cover," Sophie told Rayme as she maneuvered the heavy metal hospital bed sideways into a horizontal position facing the window. "Stay back here with me. We'll be fine."

Freitan pulled the plastic retractable blind down over the bullet-proof observation window as Matsue joined her. "Let's each cover a point of entry."

The two law enforcement agents bracketed the covered window and locked door, weapons drawn. Freitan barked into her radio, asking for information, but no one replied.

Steps thundered outside in the hallway. More shots rang out. Yelling added to the cacophony of the electronic alarm. Sophie fumbled her phone out of her pocket. She had upgraded recently to a satellite phone, but when she thumbed it on, *No Service* showed in the window. *"Foul stench of a week-old corpse."*

"What's that you're saying?" Rayme whispered. Her teeth were chattering and her eyes were wide in her bruised face. "I'm scared too."

"I curse in Thai sometimes, my native tongue," Sophie said. She held up her phone. "Either of you getting a signal over there?"

"Nope," Freitan said. "But reception's never good in this building."

"I can usually get a few bars. This is weird," Matsue said. "I'm guessing someone's got a jammer."

Sophie's heart rate was up, but she wasn't unduly alarmed. Three highly trained professionals, two of them armed, were barricaded in with Holly Rayme, and this disturbance was likely not even related to their prisoner. She smiled at Rayme. "Try to stay calm. We've got you covered."

More gunshots and deafening footsteps in the hallway were not reassuring. Neither was the shout, "Rayme's in the infirmary *somewhere*. Just start trying doors!"

The knob rattled. The door shook under pounding with some metal object. The impacts sent medical supplies piled on the shelves crashing to the floor.

Rayme let out a squeal of fear after one particularly loud smash, moving to clutch Sophie. Sophie wrapped her arms around the trembling woman. She covered Rayme's mouth with a hand. "Don't let them hear you," she whispered in Rayme's ear.

A flash of memory burst across Sophie's brain.

Sophie was the one being held in someone's arms. A hand covered her mouth. A desperate voice whispered, *"Don't let them hear you."* Suppressed memory came flooding back. Sophie's arms tightened around Rayme.

The woman holding Sophie had been her beloved nanny, Armita.

Armita had fought like a tigress when kidnappers broke into seven-year-old Sophie's room, screaming and beating at the men with a broom. Sophie's last sight of Armita had been of her nanny, head bleeding, sprawled on the ground unconscious as masked men in black carried Sophie away.

She had never seen Armita again.

After the ransom was paid and Sophie was returned, her mother told her that Armita had quit because she didn't want to work at a home where she'd be in danger. Armita had been hurt because of Sophie; and she'd left because of Sophie.

Self-blame had been a heart-splinter of Sophie's ever since. As Sophie held Holly Rayme's trembling, sweating body in her arms, she let that splinter go. *Not my fault. I was just a child.*

Another missing piece from her past to ask her mysterious mother, Pim Wat, about…

The heavy crash of something metal hitting the covered viewing window made Sophie hunch instinctively over Rayme, protecting the woman with her body, as intruders bashed at the safety glass, bowing it in and shattering it.

Sophie peeked over their crude barrier. Two lean, dark men in prison orange filled the window's opening, shoving aside the dangling blind with their hands, pushing the sheet of glass, held together by wire, out of the way.

And then, Freitan and Matsue were up and firing. Sophie and Rayme curled close, covering their ears as they hid behind the bed.

The burning, tangy scent of weapons discharge.

Ears ringing, assaulted by gunfire in a small, enclosed space.

Curses and screams.

A long moment passed as silence fell, broken by Rayme's sobbing.

Sophie lifted her head to peer out from cover. Matsue and Freitan stood in identical shooting stances, aiming their weapons at the empty, crude opening in the window.

More running, yelling, and gunfire out in the hall, this time passing by. No further incursions.

"Suspects are down." Freitan clicked the deadbolt open. "I'm going to see what's happening." She was out the door before Matsue could object.

The Marshal turned wide, tilted brown eyes upon Sophie. "You two okay?"

"Yes." Sophie tried her phone again. "The jammer is off. I've got a signal."

She dialed 911 and was told that backup was on its way and the riot was almost under control.

Rayme wriggled out of Sophie's arms and adjusted her gaping hospital gown. "Thanks. Almost seemed like you cared for a moment there."

"I always do the right thing no matter how I feel about someone personally," Sophie said. Rayme winced, then crawled back up onto the bed and pulled the sheet up over her head.

Matsue came to stand over Sophie. "If what you just said is true, then we will get along and work together just fine." She turned to Holly Rayme, still hidden under the sheet. "Your application to WITSEC is hereby approved."

CHAPTER TWO

ALIKA WOLCOTT HAD ARRIVED in Hilo yesterday, flying into the airport on his Bell Jet Ranger. On island for business, he was shopping for exotic hardwoods to put some finishing touches on his new, eco-friendly Kaua`i development.

He had been trying Sophie's phone for the last hour. She'd texted him a new number the previous week, saying only that the other phone had been broken. But as usual, he suspected there was more to it than that.

He couldn't wait to see her. When the opportunity to look for finish trim for some cabinetry materials presented itself, he took the excuse to fly to the Big Island.

Sitting in the helicopter, he monitored the police band on his radio. The band was alive with a major emergency involving the jail. Alika had been studying the law enforcement codes used in communication, interested in anything that had to do with something Sophie might be involved in.

He locked up the helicopter and walked across the tarmac to the airport area, carrying his overnight duffel, and caught a shuttle to a nearby car rental agency. He secured a work truck for three days, hopefully enough time to find the wood he needed—*and to see Sophie at least once.*

Seated in the truck, Alika tried her number again, almost a reflex; but this time, she picked up.

"Alika!" Sophie's husky voice with that accent gave him "chicken skin." He could hear noise in the background: raised voices, clattering. "I'm at the jail. There's a disturbance. This isn't a good time."

His heart rate spiked. "Are you okay? Are you safe?"

"Yes. I believe so. Though the exact extent of the riot and its aftermath are still being determined and contained."

"Holy shit! Well, I just called because I wanted to let you know that I'm on the island and would like to see you while I'm here."

There was a short pause. He could tell how distracted Sophie was by her lack of response and the brisk, "That's fine. I'll call you later. Goodbye," with which she ended the call.

Alika stared down at his phone. *Never a good idea to get his expectations up when it came to Sophie.* She'd made him no promises. He had made her none either. Too bad for him that the mere sound of her voice turned his innards to mush.

He had come here for work, and he had work to do. *Enough with the navel-gazing.*

Alika fired up the truck and programmed the address of the exotic hardwoods sawmill he had come to visit into the GPS. He'd call her tonight and take a temperature check on dinner.

CHAPTER THREE

BYRON CHANG LACED his fingers together over his belly and leaned back in his leather chair. He narrowed his eyes at his cousin Terence, seated across from him in the high-ceilinged office of the downtown Hilo warehouse building where Chang Incorporated conducted a legit import/export business. "I'm not a patient man, cuz. We need to get my bruddah out dat jail."

"I'm working on it." Terence handled legal and computer-related business for the family. "But you need to acknowledge that Akane's habits have drawn too much attention."

Terence was dressed, as usual, in hipster jeans with some kind of fancy basketball shoes and a tight black T-shirt. He looked like something out of a freakin' college catalog, and he talked like it too. "Just telling you like it is, Byron. Akane knows that we would cover him for his work for the family, but this extracurricular shit he was into...well, he's on his own for that."

Byron's mouth tightened. His brother Akane did a good job as the Chang enforcer, but doing the family's dirty work had led to an unhealthy habit of knife-stalking victims, sanctioned and unsanctioned, in the jungle. "You don't speak for the family, Terence. You gave that up when you passed on being Healani's heir."

As firstborn son of the firstborn son and bearer of the Terence Chang name, the kid in front of Byron had had it all handed to him— and Terence had turned it down, going straight with a legit online tech business and importing company. Byron had stepped up to lead after another fiasco had cleared out competition from a couple of half-cousins.

Righteous anger heated Byron's chest. Terence acted like his privileged, college-educated shit didn't stink. "Akane is my brother. Doesn't matter what he's done; we are not leaving him to rot in jail. That blonde tweaker chick and the lady private investigator are going down. With them gone, there won't be a case. Everything they have on Akane is hearsay; there's not a shred of physical evidence connecting him to any of those bodies. He was good at making sure of that."

Terence smoothed one leg of his skinny jeans, cocking an ankle on his knee. It was a wonder the asshole could move; those pants were so tight. "Akane is a liability. He's attracting heat and publicity. And even if you kill off these witnesses, he is going to need to be watched like a rabid dog. You going to be the one holding his leash? Because rabid dogs bite the hand that feeds them." Terence was talking about his own recent problems dealing with an out-of-control half brother and sister who'd gone on a revenge spree against the cop involved with their father's death.

Byron shrugged. "We aren't leaving Akane in jail. Sends a bad message." *Terence was probably right about Akane.* Loyalty was important, though, and protecting their best enforcer sent a message to those beneath them about the lengths the Chang family would go to protect their own, and their interests. "I'm listening to you, T. But all I hear is flapping lips. Until you're ready to step up and serve the family by getting your hands dirty, you have no voice here."

"I'm guessing Rayme is going into Witness Protection. And that security investigator woman that kicked Akane in the balls seems pretty capable, so you may not be able to do damage control."

Terence was still giving attitude. "I think we should just leave Akane in the system."

"And I said no. Getting rid of the witnesses is not going to be a problem." Byron knew something that Terence didn't. He smiled confidently. *His brother would be free in a week or two.*

Terence set his fancy shoes down on the polished floor and stood. "I've gone straight, but that doesn't mean I don't care about the family. You're making a mistake out of misguided loyalty. Would Akane do the same for you?" Terence held Byron's gaze. "My guess is no."

Dust spiraled in a column of light shining through one of the high old windows of the historic and functional warehouse. The building had made it through the great Hilo tsunami of 1946. It had been a Chang warehouse then, and it would still be serving them in another hundred years. Byron would protect it, and the family's interest, with his dying breath. "I don't bother with regrets or looking back, college boy. Don't watch the news if your stomach can't handle what comes next. Get gone and don't come by my office without an appointment again." Byron depressed an intercom button on his desk and said, "Lani, Terence was just leaving. Make sure my cousin gets his allowance envelope on the way out. Wouldn't want him to feel shorted from his cut of this quarter's profits."

"Yes, sir." Lani and Byron had an appointment in the book later involving her on her knees under his desk, but his assistant knew how to keep up appearances at the front end.

Terence shook his head. "I hope you're making the right call about Akane." He left, closing the door softly behind him.

Byron reached into a locked drawer in his desk and withdrew a new, unregistered cell phone. He pressed down the ON button for a pre-programmed number and put the phone to his ear. *Time to make sure those witnesses were out of the way.*

CHAPTER FOUR

P IM W AT SWAM slowly in the warm, saltwater infinity pool, looking out through the Plexiglas side that faced the ocean. The pool was built on the top floor of the Kona Royal Hawaiian Hotel, and the transparent side, so many stories up, gave a feeling of swimming through sky and sea.

She enjoyed the exotic view, the silky feel of the water on her skin. After her swim, she had a massage and facial scheduled, then calling in favors to contact the CEO of Security Solutions to locate her daughter.

Sophie Malee was proving problematic. Her female offspring was no longer the biddable, sweet child she'd been.

Pim Wat speeded up her lap, annoyance a prod to her spine. She was growing impatient with Sophie Malee's stalling about her proposal that she join their clandestine organization. *But the girl was right.* Why should she be loyal to a mother that had sold her out to that foul gangster Assan Ang? What incentive did Sophie Malee have to cooperate and get involved with the Yām Khûmkạn?

What Pim Wat needed wasn't incentive, but *leverage.* Something to force the girl to work for them. Damaging information or consequences that would ensure Sophie Malee not only came on board but didn't go to the Americans with anything she learned about the organization.

Pim Wat had a file started on Sophie back in her room, all she'd been able to assemble through the Yām Khûmkạn's spy network—and it wasn't enough.

Sophie Malee had few friends, a powerful rogue computer program, and a ridiculous dog. Two men, Jake Dunn and Alika Wolcott, were pursuing her. It had been three, but Todd Remarkian had been killed by Assan and his henchmen. Which of the remaining two Sophie preferred was difficult to determine.

Pim Wat had files on Sophie's suitors also. She had documented their habits, financials, relationships—but she hadn't yet determined their weaknesses, or how they could be used to gain Sophie's cooperation.

But she didn't want to threaten Sophie Malee until she had to. "Better to entice a monkey with fruit" was an old saying she knew to be true. Once Sophie picked a partner, the Yām Khûmkạn would have the advantage Pim Wat needed.

In the meantime, she'd get that meeting with Security Solutions' CEO and track down her daughter. The thought gave Pim Wat new energy. Her arms scythed through the water, smooth as a shark swimming.

CHAPTER FIVE

SOPHIE UNLOCKED the door of the tree house she was renting, enjoying the creaking of the branches around her and the shushing of their leaves. The platform deck on the compact, two-story tiny house swayed, a little like the deck of a boat. Twenty feet up in the center of a massive banyan tree, Sophie felt safe and soothed by the constant sounds of nature all around her.

Sophie's therapist, Dr. Wilson, had put her in touch with the owner, a woman in her sixties who operated a number of quirky, alternative dwellings on her large property just outside of Hilo. The tree house sported a composting toilet, an instant heat propane water heater, and solar operated lights and power. One of the practical features of the tree house was the hand crank dumbwaiter used to bring supplies up and down.

Sophie's yellow Lab, Ginger, had needed coaxing to deal with the daily rides up and down in an enclosed box, but she had soon gotten used to it. Sophie had already rewarded Ginger with a dog biscuit and loaded the dog inside the dumbwaiter at the bottom of the tree.

Sophie cranked the wheel that raised the crude elevator, thankful for the exertion that warmed up muscles tight from the many hours of sitting and tension that had followed the jail riot, as security protocols were followed and statements taken about the attack.

One thing was obvious: two potential killers, now dead, had targeted Holly Rayme. Rayme would have been "a sitting duck," as Sophie's friend, FBI agent Marcella Scott, would have described her, if Freitan and Matsue hadn't been on hand to defend her.

Sophie would have to remember to ask Marcella to explain that colloquialism. She'd heard it used many times and it still didn't make sense.

After letting Ginger out of the dumbwaiter and filling the dog's food and water bowls, Sophie walked through the small, compact downstairs and went up the tiny metal spiral staircase to the bedroom and bath. She turned on the photovoltaic lantern that provided the tree house's main source of illumination and shed her clothing into a hamper. She showered in the small tub surround, soaping up briskly.

As Sophie slid soapy hands over the curlicued Thai tattoos decorating her outer thighs, inner arms and navel, she remembered her partner Jake touching the markings, his big hands exquisitely gentle —and powerfully possessive.

They'd crossed a line on that last case, and she couldn't regret it. Jake had been a thoughtful, passionate lover who warmed her inside and out. He'd been able to draw her out of her depression. All of which was good—but Jake didn't want to continue as "partners with benefits." He wanted exclusivity, and she wasn't ready for that.

And to complicate things further, Alika had called.

Her MMA coach, friend and sometime boyfriend was on the island, and wanted to see her. Was it wrong that she wanted to see him too? That she had feelings for more than one man?

"Why are you in such a hurry to decide?" Dr. Wilson's wise voice spoke in her mind. "They're big boys. Just be honest about how things are for you and let the chips fall where they may."

Thankfully, Sophie had an appointment with the psychologist coming up soon. Dr. Wilson seemed to see nothing wrong with Sophie's dilemma. "You're figuring out who you are," she'd told

Sophie recently. "Each of these men appeals to a different side of you; each of them has something to give you and teach you. Don't rush the process just because it's uncomfortable."

She couldn't call Alika back yet. There was another call she needed to make, one she wasn't looking forward to.

Sophie dressed in the breathable, utilitarian hike/sleepwear she liked for the cooler temperature of the area. She heated some leftover stew, fragrant with lemongrass and seafood, and poured it over a bed of rice. She carried her dinner, along with a steaming cup of aromatic tea, to the little computer workstation she'd constructed in the corner of the minuscule bedroom.

The tree house's elevation took her up high enough to bypass any interference that might slow down her laptop's powerful satellite uplink. She was secure and safe here from any but the most sensitive spy signal equipment—and the tree house's location in an isolated commune was an additional layer of cyber protection.

She moved the slender bamboo chair aside and pulled up a corner of plywood flooring under the carpet. The narrow space hid a small daypack. She removed the square, boxy-shaped external solid-state drive that contained the Ghost software program. She plugged it into the laptop, waited for it to load, and then launched the software, battling that conflicted feeling she got whenever she had contact with the Ghost.

Connor.

Her ex-boyfriend, a man who lived under the alias of Sheldon Hamilton, CEO of Security Solutions.

Computer genius, violinist, athlete, entrepreneur, inventor, billionaire.

Vigilante.

Activating his software automatically sent Connor a message that she was online and available to communicate with. She had been interacting with him as little as possible since their breakup, but now she needed him.

Holly Rayme had been processed out of jail into Hazel Matsue's custody. The U.S. Marshal had refused to give Sophie or Freitan any further information about their location or security protocols.

"Once a client is in our custody, they're ours. I'll call you once I have Rayme settled in a safe place," she told Sophie. "We can get together and talk about how to team this. But here is where we part ways until the trial," she told Freitan at the jail.

"Understood. Keep her alive," Freitan said.

Matsue had left, towing a reluctant Rayme toward an unmarked beige Toyota 4Runner. A shadowy figure behind tinted glass showed Sophie that Matsue had further backup, and she was glad of it.

Weeks before on a hike in Kalapana's fresh lava flows, Sophie had discovered the body dump of a murdered family. Further investigation had determined that they had been in WITSEC. Matsue had boldly asserted that no witness under the Marshals Service's protection who followed safety protocols and direction had ever lost his life —but that case had uncovered a leak in the program's operation on the Big Island that had led to the family's assassination.

Sophie had contacted the Ghost about it. The Ghost specialized in dealing with the unreachable, and some sort of leak within WITSEC was just the kind of challenge he loved. He, of all people, was able to hunt down and identify a breach in the agency's security. Connor relished nothing more than to turn whoever was involved against each other using his unique computer skills and the Ghost software.

Connor had let her know he was making progress at unearthing the source of the leak, and now that Holly Rayme was Sophie's client, she needed to find out exactly what that progress was.

The photovoltaic lamp created a reflection of her face on the dark surface of the monitor, inactive but for a pulsing green cursor as she waited to see if Connor reacted to her use of his program.

Sophie studied the outline of her visage.

She'd been told she was beautiful before a recent gunshot wound had disfigured her. Now, whenever Sophie saw her face, the scar was all she noticed.

In the monitor's reflection, the shape of her face was still a pleasing oval. Her lips were full, her nose straight, her brows a symmetrical bracket above her eyes.

That was where the good news ended. Sophie's eyes were misaligned; one tilted up, one down. The extensive graft and prosthetic used to patch her shattered cheekbone had pulled the skin of her face in slightly different directions. A pink line of scarring bisected her cheek and ran all the way up into her hairline, as if she'd taken a slash from a knife or other sharp object. The color of the graft was slightly different too, the pale gold tone of skin from Sophie's hip.

Still. She should be grateful. Other than curious looks upon meeting her, people treated her normally. The three men she was close to had shown no sign of being repulsed.

The green cursor unspooled as Connor made contact. *"Sophie. Are you there?"*

"Waiting for you," she typed back. *"I need info about the WITSEC leak. My client is in the program, and I want to make sure she's safe."*

"We should talk on the phone."

But then she'd have to hear his smooth, buttery voice, and resist the feelings that voice stirred up.

Sophie had thought she loved him. He'd been the first man she'd slept with after her abusive husband. They'd begun a relationship she thought was going somewhere special and permanent.

And then he'd betrayed her.

Sophie was never going to let it go, because his behavior pointed to a deeper problem: he'd never love her as much as he loved his vigilantism as the Ghost.

"No phone. This is fine. Tell me what you've found out." Their chat function was untraceable, and actually better than a phone conversation in that way.

"I've confirmed that there's a leak in the Hawaii branch of Witness Protection. The Marshals keep their witness locations secret,

but within a framework of known and vetted safe houses. Once a witness is out of active custody, they are supposed to maintain a low profile under their new identity and not make any contact with their old life. In the case of the Jones family whose bodies you were unfortunate enough to find, the mother had taken an unauthorized shopping trip to Oahu and broke protocol. Her activity was logged and may have been what triggered the leak.

The security breach begins with a RAT attached to the Hawaii WITSEC server. The information is then sold to the witness's enemies by a dirty agent via Tor. I am not able to identify who the agent is: the harvesting computer is masked by multiple VPNs. But this is someone with computer skills who is doing a good job of covering their tracks within the agency, and even keeping the leak secret by hiding it behind protocol violations."

Sophie could picture Connor's chiseled features in the glow of a monitor somewhere, his fingers flying on the keys as he talked to her in a language they both understood. A RAT was a Remote Access Trojan, a burrowing program that could turn any computer into a spy device. VPNs were Virtual Private Networks, a way of scrambling a location by bouncing it off different servers, and Tor referred to accessing the "dark net" of untraceable sites.

Sophie responded. *"I'm now working with an agent to guard my client. Client's name is Holly Rayme. Agent's name is Hazel Matsue. I've been hired by several families of the Chang victims to make sure Rayme lives long enough to testify against Akane Chang. I'll be in a position to surveil Matsue, at least."* Sophie gazed up and to the left, considering. *"I could put DAVID to work on coming up with parallels between the cases that were leaked/breached. See if there are any patterns."*

"Good idea. I can send you a file with the witnesses lost that are likely a result of the RAT."

"That would make my work easier. Why can't you shut down the RAT?" A good programmer could deploy countermeasures that

would disable such a virus, and Sophie was surprised that Connor hadn't done so.

"I could. But then, the operator would know someone was onto him, and would find some other way to do business. This is perfect. You and I will work together to uncover the dirty agent, then we can eliminate the RAT."

No. Sophie wasn't partnering with Connor on anything. *"My focus is narrow. I am concerned only with protecting my client."*

"I don't believe that, Sophie. I saw photos of the Jones family's massacre. You must want what happened to them to be stopped."

Sophie frowned.

Connor was right. She saw the little Jones girl's pecked-out eyes every time she thought of the case. She typed back rapidly. *"Let's begin here and see where this goes. I have a meeting with Matsue tomorrow at noon. I will ingratiate myself."*

"Darling Sophie, you are many things, but not ingratiating. Just be yourself. And if that fails and she won't work with you, you can just work with me."

He was right that she wasn't good at ingratiating herself. People either liked her or they didn't. *"I will do that anyway, given my alleged lack of socialization."* Sophie paused. *"Where are you?"*

"Does it matter?"

"I would like to know if you are in Hawaii." The FBI was still after the Ghost. She hadn't expected that he would come back to the United States anytime soon, if ever.

"I'm in Thailand. Very interesting, your country of origin. Corruption is rife. I'm very busy."

Her heart thundered. She placed a palm over it to still its galloping.

It couldn't be a coincidence that her estranged mother, Pim Wat, had so recently contacted her with an outrageous proposal; the stated reason for that was that Thailand's government was under attack via technology. *Was Connor involved?* Would working for her mother's clandestine organization, the Yām Khûmkạn, pit her against the Ghost?

She still needed to contact her ambassador father, Frank Smithson, and his Secret Service agent, Ellie Smith, about her mother's spying.

"I will proceed with caution and get back to you soon. Hopefully we can identify the security breach quickly," Sophie typed. She wasn't about to let Connor know about her mother's bizarre visit and proposal about joining the secret group.

"And then we'll plug the leak. Permanently," the Ghost typed back. *"We'll do what no one else can."*

He was appealing to her vanity, trying to paint them as a team. Sophie chose to ignore that baiting comment. *"Thank you for taking the case,"* Sophie typed. *"I have always understood the reason why you do what you do."*

"Anything for you, Sophie."

"Don't. Just don't, Connor." All the confusion• Sophie was feeling about the men in her life rose up in a rush of resentment. *"You had your chance with me, and you blew it up. Literally. Take this case because it's the right thing to do. No other reason."*

"I do what I want, for whom I want, when I want. It's called freedom, and it's a rare elixir few can afford. Goodbye, Sophie."

The green cursor chat box winked out.

CHAPTER SIX

ALIKA FACED Sophie from across a heavily lacquered wooden table in a little breakfast café in Hilo. The ambiance of a busy restaurant swirled around them: the chatter of customers, the smell of coffee brewing, the clash of dishes in the back.

Sophie doused her Lipton tea bag in a thick china cup. Alika tried not to be obvious about staring at her, but it was hard. He was starved to see her, touch her, know everything about what she'd been through since he dropped her off for her hike just a few weeks ago.

Sophie was on the thin side of what looked best on her—every muscle tightly defined and her cheekbones hollow. The scar on her face seemed to have settled into whatever it was going to be; the vivid red line was fading, and the color change of the skin graft had become less noticeable as it healed and she got sun exposure on the new skin.

She was still too beautiful for her own good.

A little twist of disgust tightened Sophie's full lips, the expression of a dedicated tea drinker faced with an inferior beverage. He smiled as she dipped the tea bag repeatedly. "I'm glad you could make the time to see me."

She smiled back. "I will always make time to see you, Alika."

That didn't make his pulse pick up at all. "You said you had a pretty eventful case recently. And it's continuing."

"Correct. I had a week to do some sightseeing with my partner Jake when phase one of the case wrapped, but then I was retained again. Now I'm providing security for an endangered witness."

"Sounds dangerous."

Sophie shrugged. "The Witness Protection Program is carrying most of the responsibility."

"So, what's today like?" Alika didn't want to push his luck. She had been distant on the phone during the last few weeks; in fact, ever since he had dropped her off on the black lava plain of Kalapana after their Kaua`i adventure, he'd felt her drifting away.

"I'm free until about noon. That's why I could meet with you. I am having lunch with the U.S. Marshal working my case later, but if you wanted to take a run from here up to Rainbow Falls, I've always wanted to see it and haven't had a chance to go."

Their breakfast arrived, and Alika grinned at the giant spread of eggs, fried rice, Portuguese sausage and pineapple slices. He gestured with his chin to Sophie's loaded plate. "We're going to be moving slowly after this crazy pile of food."

"Fine with me. I've been burning the candle at both ends lately, as they say." Sophie picked up her fork and dug in.

He sneaked another glance. *She needed the calories.* "You're looking good, Sophie."

"I am not. I haven't been caring for myself. But I appreciate the compliment."

"You're just a little raggedy around the edges. I hope you're planning to change that. Or I might have to come over here and keep an eye on you." He spoke jokingly, but Sophie's eyes widened with alarm.

"I am not ready to be in a relationship right now. I told Jake the same thing."

Jake. That testosterone-driven asshole with his over-the-top

26

Special Forces stories. The dude probably spent the whole two weeks he'd been working with Sophie trying to get her into bed.

"So you had that talk with Jake, did you?" Alika shook salt onto his eggs for something to do.

"I think Jake is in love with me. It's very confusing." Sophie continued to shovel in her breakfast.

Alika froze, his fork poised. *Trust Sophie to say something so unvarnished and real.* "Confusing? In what way?" Alika took a bite and made himself chew. He kept his eyes down so he didn't reveal too much and spook her.

"Confusing. Because I have feelings. For both of you." Sophie had finished half of her breakfast. She set down her fork and looked him in the eye as she picked up her mug of tea. "I care too much to lie to you, Alika. Jake and I got physically involved during our case. But he wanted more than that, and I didn't. So that ended."

Alika's gut tightened so abruptly that he felt queasy. *She had slept with Jake.* And as much as Sophie meant to him, as he hoped that she cared for him too, they'd never been together that way. *He'd never had more than a few kisses in all the years they'd spent together.*

"Wow." Alika set down his fork and picked up his coffee mug, wrapping both hands around it. The sight of his brown-skinned fingers against the white mug and the warmth of the china seeping into his flesh stabilized him. "Well. I'm not going to lie. Hearing that sucks, because I was hoping we were headed toward being together after our case on Kaua`i."

"I'm sorry to hurt you." Sophie's honey-brown eyes were wide and earnest. "I am trying to be as honest and straightforward as I can. I care for you greatly. It is different from how I care for Jake. And for…" She bit her lips, stifling something she was about to say. She looked down at her fingers wrapped around her own mug. "We can be together, but only if you accept that this is where I am right now in my life. I don't know where I will be, physically or emotionally, even next week. If you can accept that there are secrets and things I can't tell you, and if you can accept that you are not the only man I care for...then we can be together, to the degree that leaves us."

The pain took a moment to register, like a blow to the solar plexus when landed by a good opponent: the recipient was paralyzed for a moment, the air blasted out of him, his body sending a signal that a severe disruption had occurred that the brain couldn't yet interpret.

Alika stood abruptly. He pulled out his wallet and threw several twenties onto the table. "You made no promises. I made no promises. We broke up. But that's a hell of a lot of 'ifs' in one sentence."

"You don't have to answer right away." Sophie hadn't moved. Her eyes looked soft, pleading. "You can think about it and get back to me."

"I need some fresh air. If I'm still outside when you finish your breakfast, we can run to the falls together." Alika spun and walked out.

The glass door tinkled as he exited the building. He walked blindly to the end of the café and turned, striding around it into the narrow graveled alley behind the restaurant. Once out of sight of the busy street, Alika cursed, coloring the air with every foul word he'd learned in a lifetime. He kicked the big green dumpster behind the bistro a couple of times, shadow-punching the air; wishing he could punch Jake, and her ex-husband, and that boyfriend she'd had who'd died. Damn them all to hell for messing her up further.

Immediate frustration discharged; grateful he had not attracted any attention, Alika went into one of his martial arts routines.

When in doubt, work it out. One of his favorite coaching sayings.

The discipline of the choreographed movements, the challenging nature of the spins, kicks and turns grounded Alika, calmed him. He wasn't in control of much—but he would manage himself, and that was enough.

When he had completed that round, he began another one.

Alika spotted Sophie out of the corner of his eye. She'd walked into the alley, her dog at her side. She was leaning against the corner of the diner, watching him.

She had not accepted that he was gone. She had come looking for him.

New energy flowed into Alika as he completed the *tae kwon do* sequence, ending it with a showy roundhouse kick and spin combo. Catching his breath, he closed his eyes and folded his hands. He bowed in her direction.

He opened his eyes.

Sophie stood straight as a slender coconut palm, hands loose at her sides but for the one grasping Ginger's leash. Her eyes were suspiciously shiny, but all she said was, "Do you still want to take a run to Rainbow Falls?"

"I'll take what I can get," he said, and walked toward her.

CHAPTER SEVEN

S<small>OPHIE RAN</small> beside Alika through the residential warren of streets on the inland side of Hilo, keeping her breath as even as possible, though her former coach set a blistering pace. Ginger was beginning to lag when they arrived at the Rainbow Falls parking lot, filled with rental cars and parked tourist buses. Close to Hilo, spectacular Rainbow Falls was a popular destination because it was near the town and accessible to even the most handicapped visitors.

Sophie followed Alika as they jogged around the milling crowds to the furthest overlook area, a concrete platform between two huge mango trees. She bent over at the waist, her hands on her knees, trying to calm nausea brought on by eating a heavy breakfast and running hard shortly afterward.

"We can walk on the way back." Alika wasn't nearly as winded as she was, even after his vigorous routine in the alley behind the restaurant. His warm brown skin gleamed in the sleeveless shirt he wore as he leaned his elbows on the barrier, gazing at the falls. Sophie's gaze traced the contours of his arms, banded by Polynesian tribal tattoos in triangular patterns.

Sophie turned and rested her arms on the cool metal railing. The scene gradually soothed Sophie and slowed her heart rate. Water gushed over the high rim of a cliff, cascading with a roar to fall eighty feet into a deep, round pool. Heliconia, *ti* leaf and various other tropical plantings rimmed the area in pleasing array. A rainbow glowed at the foaming base of the cascade.

She pointed. "I see why the falls has that name."

Alika nodded. "Classic scene. We have some beauties like this on Kaua'i, too, but not so close to a city as this. No wonder the tourists love it."

After the intensity of the conversation in the restaurant, just finding their way to some normal interaction felt good.

Sophie had exited the diner after finishing her breakfast to discover Alika had disappeared. She shivered a little, remembering the shock of pain she'd felt at seeing the sidewalk empty. She'd walked to the Jeep she'd leased. Inside, Ginger whined and scratched at the window. Sophie had decided she would walk the dog and try to work the tension out of her own muscles—and maybe she'd find Alika somehow. She'd leashed the Lab, and Ginger towed Sophie straight into the alley.

The sight of Alika whirling, punching and kicking through one of his martial arts routines had stopped her in her tracks.

Alika was a beautiful man inside and out. The devastating attack more than a year ago had left him in a coma with broken bones; but, after months of rehab and working with a special trainer, he had reclaimed power and grace. She could watch the way the sun gleamed on his muscles as he moved all day long. Knowing how hard he'd worked and how much he'd lost because of her ex-husband's insane jealousy made witnessing the strength he'd regained even sweeter.

Challenging as this situation was to navigate, she couldn't have lived with lying to him about her involvement with Jake, or her decision to stay unattached.

After taking in the Rainbow Falls scene for a few minutes more, and refreshing with some water, they turned and headed back toward town at a leisurely pace.

Sophie's stomach was finally settling after the exertion of the run and the large meal. Alika's hand swung loose beside her, and she reached out to hook a forefinger around his, not quite holding his hand, but touching and connected nonetheless. "I'm sorry if I hurt you."

"Better than being lied to, even by omission." Alika's warm brown eyes were steady. *He was always steady.* Even when he was hurting, he would never direct that hurt at her. "Tell me straight if it's worth my time staying a few extra days on island so we can spend some time together."

"I would love that. But I'm working. We will have to see each other when we can fit it in." She laced her fingers with his, happy that he'd allowed the small contact.

"I'm working too—hunting for wood." Alika described the reason he had come to the Big Island. It was difficult to locate enough of the rare native *koa* hardwood he wanted for the finishing touches he had planned for a series of exclusive bungalows.

Listening to his building business challenges was a refreshing contrast to the kinds of things Sophie was dealing with. She enjoyed the mellow sound of his voice, the lilt of pidgin in the background of his speech as he told her about the underground network needed to find enough of the right wood. "It's always a guy who knows a guy who had a tree fall on his land," Alika said. "So I end up going out to these interesting places and haggling with people for cash."

"But you don't harvest the wood? There's no lumberyard that specializes in it or a place that grows it?"

"Yes, you can buy it at the lumberyard. But it's thirty to sixty dollars a board foot, and they don't usually have enough. *Koa* is protected, so the only wood available is from natural deadfalls. It's a hardwood, so trees take twenty-five or more years to grow to a decent size. The wood's a limited resource, and only getting scarcer."

"There were a lot of trees in the area where I was hiking during my last case," Sophie said. She thought of the dense jungle where Akane Chang had taken her. Her skin crawled at the memory of the man's touch, and she let go of Alika's hand to rub her arms briskly. *Whatever they needed to do to keep that man incarcerated had to be done.* That reminded her of the upcoming meeting with Matsue. She took out her phone. "I must hurry. My next appointment is coming up."

They broke into a jog.

Back at the Jeep near the restaurant, Alika lifted Sophie's hand to kiss her knuckles. The warm, sensual touch moved through her like lightning. "I'll text you this evening. Maybe we can get dinner."

"I'll cook for you in my tree house," Sophie said impulsively.

"Tree house?" His brows arched. "This I gotta see."

"Yes, and I would like to show it to you. My abode is most unusual. Small, but has everything Ginger and I need. I will let you know when we can meet. I will lead you there; the location is obscure." Their hands were still linked, and this time she kissed Alika's knuckles, and held his gaze as she did so. "Thank you for not giving up on me."

CHAPTER EIGHT

Sophie slid into the booth across from Hazel Matsue. "How is our witness?"

"Good. Safe. And that's the important thing." Matsue's asymmetrical bob swung forward, sleek and tidy, as she perused the restaurant's menu. Matsue's innate stylishness made the white tee with jeans, and a red cotton vest that concealed her weapon and badge, look like a fashion statement. "Ms. Rayme is rather vocal when she's uncomfortable. And she is uncomfortable at the moment."

"How? In what way?" Sophie accepted a slightly greasy laminated menu from an approaching waitress. This restaurant was across town from where she'd breakfasted with Alika. Her belly was still full, though, from that heavy meal. She ordered an iced tea.

"Rayme is through the worst of the withdrawals, but still craving. She misses that dead dysfunctional boyfriend of hers. And she is isolated from other human contact, and without a phone."

"I have experienced some of what you are describing on my last case. I was in Kalalau, on a solo hike, and had a taste of everything but the withdrawals. It was indeed uncomfortable."

"Well." Matsue took out a manila file and a ballpoint pen and slid the items across to Sophie. "Let's stay focused on the purpose for this meeting. I ran your background by my supervisor, and we're a go for you to help provide support on security with this case. Here is an interagency agreement for working with you and Security Solutions. We can't share the witness's location, but we can collaborate on keeping her safe and managing her until the trial, and even beyond if you like."

"The relatives of victims who joined together to pay for my services through Security Solutions were only concerned with seeing this case through to trial. Do we have a court date yet?" Sophie flipped open the file and scanned the contract.

"Freitan and Wong, as well as WITSEC, have been pushing for an expedited court date. But the Chang attorney is pushing back just as hard. He has filed for a change of venue out of this state. That would push things back considerably."

"Then I hope that doesn't go through. Although there could be advantages to taking Rayme off the island." Sophie signed the document in her rounded, back-slanting hand.

"Moving Rayme has merit, but we are always looking at the bottom line. For now, this is as good as it gets. Now, what can *you* do to help shore up her security?" Hazel Matsue took the contract file back, and eyed Sophie.

"I have access to some cutting-edge tech we can use to keep working the case and looking for more info on the threat to Rayme." Sophie bit her tongue on mentioning anything about the WITSEC leak. She could hardly disclose that massive problem at their first meeting. *Matsue might even be the dirty agent.* "I'm the one who put together the pattern of missing persons connected to Akane Chang. And I'm actually one of the only other eyewitnesses besides Rayme who can testify against Chang."

"What about the young woman you and your partner were looking for? Julie something?"

"Julie Weathersby. Security Solutions spoke to her parents about obtaining WITSEC protection, but they decided they didn't want to risk letting her out of their sight. Against our advice, they decided to hide her somewhere on the mainland until the trial, and they hired a firm that specializes in bodyguard work to protect her. They're convinced that they can keep her safe until they bring her back to testify. I just hope they're right."

"In that case, I suppose we have no choice but to proceed as if you and Holly Rayme are, at least as far as we're concerned, the only two witnesses. Has it occurred to you that you should take some security precautions as well?" Matsue's elegant brows rose in concerned arcs over her intelligent dark eyes.

"I am fine." The last thing Sophie wanted was more scrutiny, of any kind. "I have been living under security protocols for years now."

Matsue tipped her head. Her expression reminded Sophie of an inquisitive bird. "I read your file, but perhaps you want to fill me in on a few more details."

"That could take a while." The waitress arrived to take their order. Sophie asked for a small salad and strip steak for protein, still full from earlier. When the waitress left, Sophie contemplated the marshal.

Building trust with Matsue might begin through self-disclosure. "I don't know how thorough the background was that you checked, but I recently escaped death at the hands of my abusive ex-husband by killing him."

Matsue's mouth opened in surprise. "All I had was your work record and a background check."

"There has been a lot more than that going on this year." Sophie sipped the iced tea the waitress had dropped off and filled Matsue in on recent events. "I doubt I'll be on the Changs' radar as a target."

"I hope you are right."

The women's food arrived. Sophie watched the marshal from under her lashes as Matsue ate her meal of grilled fish and vegetables with precise, tidy movements. The woman radiated a calm confidence that Sophie found reassuring and attractive.

"Tell me how you became a marshal," Sophie asked. "Why that branch of law enforcement?"

Matsue smiled. "I could ask you the same, and I will someday. But for today, I'll just tell you that I'm from a family of brothers. Four of them. I am the second to the youngest. Throughout my childhood, my brothers were in sports and martial arts, and though our parents wanted me to behave more like a traditional Japanese girl of good family, I refused. I copied everything my brothers did; I fought with, competed with, and played with them. My parents finally gave in and allowed me to have all the same lessons and activities. I majored in Criminal Justice in college, and have always wanted a career busting bad guys. I liked the autonomy, travel, and diverse kinds of assignments the Marshals Service offered over other agencies."

"I understand. Your range of duties does seem interesting. I am surprised that in my experiences, I haven't worked more closely with the Marshals Service. But then, my five years in the FBI were spent mostly in the computer lab, and I've only been a private operative for a short time." Sophie gave a thumbnail sketch of her unusual career. "It's still evolving, day by day."

"Certainly never gets dull, does it? Except that I have to get back to babysitting detail with Rayme. Let me get this." Matsue picked up the check. "Let's communicate daily."

"Sounds good. And maybe when you get to know me better you'll trust me to help you with Rayme at her secret location. I know you can't leave her alone for long. It must be tiresome."

"You have no idea." Matsue rolled her eyes. "But it's protocol. Sorry. We'll talk tomorrow." Matsue picked up the file, paid the check, and the women said goodbye.

Out on the sidewalk, Sophie checked her phone—it was only two p.m. She had time to go to the South Hilo PD station and do some work with DAVID before she went to the store to pick up something to cook for dinner for Alika at the tree house.

CHAPTER NINE

Sᴏᴘʜɪᴇ ɢʀᴇᴇᴛᴇᴅ the watch officer at South Hilo station, a small storefront opening in a run-down area of Hilo. "How are you today, Officer Tito?"

The mountainous officer was hunched over his Sudoku pad. "Not too bad, Hacker Babe." His grin showed a gold tooth.

Sophie laughed. She wasn't offended, but she also didn't want that nickname to catch on. "You can just refer to me as Ms. Ang, please." She signed the visitor log and surrendered her weapon. "I'll be in the computer lab if Detective Freitan or Wong want to check in about something."

"Got it, Ms. Ang." He bounced his brows.

Sophie wended her way through the crowded cubicles of the bullpen work area. An agreement Security Solutions had worked out with the Hilo PD on her last case allowed her to use the computer lab's secure internet access to do police-related investigation work online.

The dim, cool back room with its U-shaped table of outdated computers was empty, as usual. Sophie unwound a coil of blue internet cable and plugged in her laptop. She logged into the Data Assessment Victim Information Database program that she'd developed while in the FBI. DAVID worked by data-mining online cases and other information, sifting through available information looking for keywords, then using an algorithm to test hypotheses and assign confidence ratios.

Sophie opened DAVID and checked the data collection caches she had set up monitoring the correlation between missing people and suspicious deaths. Many of these cases had been circumstantially connected to possible murders committed by Akane Chang, enforcer for the Chang family, and, it turned out, recreational serial killer. She dragged and dropped various elements into a cohesive format and saved the data to share with Matsue.

Her new burner phone rang, buzzing in her pocket. Sophie checked the caller ID and smiled as she answered. "Hello, Jake."

"Hey, Soph. What's cookin', good lookin'?"

Sophie smiled, a glow warming her at the sound of her partner and sometime lover's upbeat, energetic tone. *Jake Dunn could fill a room with his presence even through her phone.*

But she could not answer that what she was cooking was dinner for Alika without causing a negative reaction. "I have been approved to work with the U.S. Marshals on Holly Rayme's security," she told Jake instead.

"That's excellent. I guess. Except it means you're there longer." Jake sighed dramatically. "I thought I would check in about how things are going, and let you know I miss you. I'm pining. Terribly. Tank is, too." They'd rescued Holly Rayme's big-hearted pit bull on their case together, and Jake had adopted the dog and taken him back to Oahu.

"Ginger and I miss you both, as well." It was perfectly true. She still tossed and turned at night, missing his big body with its furnace-like warmth. She probably should never have been with him, but she couldn't regret it. "Things seem to be settling. Except for the prison riot."

"What?" Jake shouted. "The what?"

Sophie filled him in on the attack that had occurred at the jail.

"It certainly confirmed that Rayme needed to be taken into protective custody. Marshal Matsue took her out of there quickly after that."

"I'll bet." Concern vibrated in his tone. "And how are you doing, through all that?"

"I can hear you thinking, Jake. I was never in any real danger. Matsue and Freitan took quick and deadly action to protect Rayme. As a civilian in the jail, I was unarmed, but Rayme and I were perfectly safe hiding behind her hospital bed."

"Perfectly safe. During a prison riot. Hiding behind a hospital bed." He snorted. "I'll have to take your word for it. How is the tree house?"

"I know you thought a tree house was a crazy choice, but I still love it two weeks in. Ginger is less excited about her daily lift up and down in the dumbwaiter, but she is getting used to it."

"Glad to hear that part, at least. I did call for an additional purpose. There's someone bugging the agency to have you call her. Won't leave a name, but it's an international number. Bix told me to contact you and pass it on."

That had to be Pim Wat.

Sophie had received a strange proposal from her estranged mother a few weeks before. Her phone had been destroyed in the attack by Chang and she had been able to retrieve some of her contacts, but Pim Wat's number had not been among them.

Procrastination would have to come to an end. She was going to need to deal with this, but she wanted more pieces in place first. She needed to contact her father and his Secret Service Agent, Ellie Smith. Once she had a plan with them, she would get in touch with Pim Wat.

"Give me the number. And if this person calls back, tell her I will be in touch when I'm ready."

Jake rattled off the digits. "Mind telling me what this is about?"

"Family business. Private."

"Oh. Must be your mom, then. That's what I thought when I first got the number." Hurt that she wouldn't talk more about the subject deepened his voice.

"Yes. My wonderful mother." Sophie forced a laugh that stuck in her throat. Pim Wat's first contact with Sophie in nine years had come during her recent case with Jake. He had been present to see how devastated Sophie had been by her mother's callous treatment. "I'm sorry you had to deal with me while I was...upset."

"I'm not a bit sorry, Sophie. I'll be there for you anytime you need me. Any way you need me." Jake's voice was rough.

Sophie cleared her throat, remembering Jake's unique and effective way of getting her out of that depressive state. "I'll be in touch soon." She ended the call.

She had tried to be as upfront with Jake as she'd been with Alika. That didn't mean that either of them appreciated or liked the boundaries she was setting.

Sophie went to the computer lab door and locked it. She wanted absolute privacy for the next call she needed to make.

CHAPTER TEN

Sᴏᴘʜɪᴇ ʜᴀᴅ last spoken to Secret Service agent Ellie Smith a year or so previously about a security breach to Sophie's ambassador father that Sophie had been involved in. Ellie had a crisp, no-nonsense tone. "What can I help you with, Sophie?"

"I have something very important to speak with you and Dad about."

"That sounds ominous."

"I want to tell you two together because it's both personal and professional. Very serious, and the situation involves national security." Sophie shut her eyes and covered them with a hand, hunching over the phone, hoping no one would pound on the locked door of the Hilo PD computer lab. "Even with all my law enforcement contacts, calling you is the best way to deal with this that I could imagine."

She could almost hear the frown in Smith's voice. "That does sound serious. How do you want to proceed? Can you come to Oahu and meet with us? Your father is on island at the moment."

"If it's at all possible, I need you both to come to the Big Island. Keep a low profile. I think I'm being watched."

"And that isn't dramatic at all." Ellie sounded skeptical.

"I am not exaggerating. Please take this seriously. You can reach me at this number." Sophie rattled off the number for her latest burner phone.

Her phone call to her father went smoothly, but only because he didn't pick up. "I hope you will find time to come over to meet with me, Dad. I already called Agent Smith. I can't say more until I'm with you and Ellie in person. This matter is time sensitive so please…come soon."

She was too agitated after that to settle to do any more work. A glance at her phone showed four p.m. She could take Ginger for a run, pick up some food, and be ready to meet Alika near his hotel to guide him to the tree house. She knew better than to try to tell him how to get to the compound's obscure jungle location.

"THIS. I LOVE THIS." Alika's grin showed perfect white teeth as he spread his arms to encompass the huge spread of the banyan tree's limbs and the view of tropical forest and mountain to be had from the tree house's tiny deck. He turned to her, arms still open. "You knew I would love this."

"I felt confident that, as a builder, you would appreciate both the aesthetic and functional aspects of my new abode." Sophie finished cranking Ginger up from the ground and the Lab jumped out of the dumbwaiter onto the swaying deck.

"You talk like a professor when you're nervous, Sophie," Alika teased. "But you're right. I appreciate."

"You think I'm nervous?" Sophie unlocked the tree house's door, gesturing for him to follow her. "It's just the first time I have cooked for a man in my own home."

"Really?" She heard pleasure in Alika's voice as they each carried in a shopping bag.

"Really." Sophie unloaded the shopping bag she'd brought up, laying the ingredients for a vegetable and beef stir-fry on the counter.

"What about that guy you dated on Oahu? Todd Remarkian?"

Sophie filled the tiny rice cooker and plugged it in. "Todd never came over to my own apartment in Honolulu. When I was injured, he stayed with me at my father's. Sometimes I stayed at his place, or we went out. In general, I do not cook." Sophie rinsed the herbs and vegetables and began chopping them. "Would you like a beer? I brought some Kirin to go with the meal."

"Sure."

She popped the tops on two of the bottled beverages and handed one of them to Alika.

"To new experiences with old friends." Alika clinked his bottle to hers.

Friends. It wasn't the first time he'd defined their relationship that way. Did he want more, after her declaration earlier in the day? Did she? She sipped her beer. *Friends was good enough for now.*

Alika turned in the tiny living room, looking at the view showcased by the picture window. "This is really tight and well put together. Do you mind if I have a look around? I want to see all the work the designer has done in making every inch of this place useful."

"Of course." Sophie heated the wok on her tiny propane stove. She took a moment to feed Ginger her kibble, listening to the creak of Alika's footsteps overhead as he walked around.

In her bedroom. And her bathroom. Around her little office.

It actually felt good to her to have him here, to know he was in her most private spaces, filling them with his calm, supportive company.

How could she have such strong feelings for more than one man? Was she broken in some way, defective, twisted? Had Assan ruined her? How was she going to ever get out of this strange situation?

She chopped harder, trying to silence the buzz of mental questions.

She had never trusted Connor enough to invite him to her Mary Watson apartment, but she'd enjoy showing Jake this place—she could easily picture his enthusiasm, the way he'd heft himself up and down the tiny staircase with a couple of swings of his arms and body, his excited energy filling the small rooms in a very different way than Alika's presence did.

She tossed the vegetables and cubed steak into the wok. Sesame oil spattered and burned the skin of her arm. *"Tiger balls!"* Sophie dropped the tongs.

"You okay?" Alika peered down the spiral staircase, frowning in concern. "Need some help?"

"Just a little hot oil. I'm fine." Sophie busied herself with tossing the stir-fry.

Alika came back down the ladder, and Ginger greeted him with a happy woof. He caressed the dog's ears. "I love the space management. Attractive and functional," he pronounced.

"It is all I need. You can wash at the sink." Sophie served the stir-fry into large pressed bamboo bowls over rice. She gestured to the tiny round table and they sat.

He picked up his chopsticks, took a bite and rolled his eyes as he chewed. "Delicious."

Sophie's neck heated at the compliment. "The lemongrass is something I remember from growing up in Thailand."

"Tell me more about that. You've never talked about your past." Alika took a sip of his beer.

"I never had occasion to talk about it because you and I were always at Fight Club, training—hardly the place for reminiscing. But there's not much to discuss. I had an unusual childhood because I had unusual parents." Sophie pointed her bottle at him. "I know little about your family, either. Except that they are beautiful people of Hawaiian origin, and you are from Kaua`i."

"Not full Hawaiian. I'm half Caucasian, and my biological father wouldn't acknowledge me. I was adopted later by my mother's husband, Sean Wolcott. You met him at the hospital." Yes, Sophie had met Alika's parents during those tense hours he'd been in a coma —*not the best time to be introduced as his girlfriend.* "You are not going to get me off the topic by deflecting. Tell me more about growing up in Thailand." Alika ate with enthusiasm, and Sophie liked watching him do so.

She took a bite and chewed deliberately, closing her eyes to access memory. "I spent the first twelve years of my life in a very traditional setting in Thailand, our family's home on the Ping River near Bangkok. The house was high up on stilts in case of flooding by the river, which happened most winters. Built of native wood with many rooms, the dwelling was designed around a raised central courtyard area where our family gathered for meals and socializing." Sophie paused to sip her beer. "Each family unit in the compound had its own apartments, I guess you would call them. My aunts took turns cooking; or I should say, supervising meals that servants cooked for the whole family." Sophie lowered her eyes to her bowl, swamped with memories of the rich sounds, smells, and culture of her homeland. "We were a wealthy family by the standards of the area. And it was a good life, for the most part, until my parents divorced. After the divorce, I went to boarding school in Geneva, Switzerland."

"Seasons. That must've been a shock." Alika got up and refilled his bowl from the wok. "Just having four seasons must have been weird. I spent some time in Colorado going to college, and I found it challenging after living in Hawaii my whole life."

"It was strange, indeed. But my father insisted. He wanted me to be prepared to be a dual citizen of the West as well as Thailand. I was twelve—not a baby any more. My mother could not care for me, and my aunts were too busy with their own families to help."

"Why couldn't your mother care for you? Same reason she didn't supervise the cooking?" Alika was making rapid progress on his second bowl of stir-fry.

"She was crippled by depression. A sickness of the spirit." Her mother was a closed door, a whispered "she's not well," and a sad, empty, unresponsive gaze.

Pim Wat's depression had resulted in her complete withdrawal from her child and her marriage—but how much of that was real? Now that she knew her mother was actually an operative for an ancient and mysterious organization, every childhood memory had to be seen through a different lens.

How many times had Pim Wat actually been involved with some secret mission while supposedly ill in bed?

Alika stared at Sophie. His bowl was already empty. "Why didn't you ever talk about this before?"

"I was too busy trying to recover from the things I went through with my ex-husband to think much about the things I went through with my family in Thailand. That took a distant second in the forefront of my mind. I am a private person. I don't like to talk about my family." Sophie met Alika's gaze. "But I want you to know something about why I am the way I am. Why it's hard for me to connect with people."

Alika rested his hand over hers on the little table. "Your dad, Frank, seems like a good guy." The Ambassador and Alika had met on Oahu a few times over the years. "He was right to prepare you to be an international citizen."

"Without him...I don't know where I would be." Sophie bit her lip. Her father had been too busy to know all the ways Sophie had suffered under her mother's indifference, but he'd done all he could. Boarding school had been the best possible setting for Sophie. She'd been able to discover her love of sports, languages and technology there. "I don't like to dig up the past."

Alika picked up her hand. Large and brown, his was calloused across the palm from construction work. "I don't take your trust for granted." He stroked her palm with his thumb, sending a tingle straight to her heart.

Sophie pulled away. She got up and cleared the dishes into the minuscule sink. "Let's go into the living room to finish our drinks, and you can tell me about *your* life, growing up on Kaua`i."

CHAPTER ELEVEN

ALIKA COULD FEEL the barrier between him and Sophie, an invisible wall. He'd nearly lost her completely since they'd broken up. She'd been intimate with other men in the meantime. *But she had invited him to her home, and made him a meal, and it was the first time she had done that for anyone.* He suspected she didn't often talk about her childhood, either.

He carried his beer into the tiny front room, admiring the excellence of the tree house's construction and the shadows of the leaves against the midnight sky through the picture window. Whoever this builder was had done a good job.

Sophie joined him at the window. "The moon is rising." She pointed to a faint glow in the dark sky above the lacy scrim of black tree line.

A high-pitched *peew!* and the sound of breaking glass seemed to occur simultaneously. Alika felt wetness cascade over his hand. He stared down in disbelief at beer foaming out of the remains of the shattered bottle he held. Warm night breeze wafted through a circular hole the size of his fist in the window in front of him.

What had just happened?

Sophie slammed into him and bore him to the ground. Her strong, solid weight pinned him to the wooden floor. "Stay down!"

Any other reason for being on the floor beneath Sophie would have made him happy, but not her trying to protect him with her body. Alika shoved at her. "Let me up!"

"Are you hurt?"

"No, dammit! Get off me!" He pushed at her shoulder.

"Someone's shooting at us."

Ginger barked, and that got Sophie's attention. She rolled off of Alika, heading in a crouch for the Lab, who was standing at the door, barking and waving her tail.

"No shit, someone's shooting at us." Alika rolled up to his knees, staying tucked beneath the level of the window.

Peew!

This time, the entire window collapsed in a shower of glittering debris. Alika ducked his head and shut his eyes as slivers cascaded over him in a lethally sharp rain.

Sophie hit the switch by the door, extinguishing the lights. Darkness fell, punctuated by the sound of Ginger panting.

"Are you all right?" Sophie whispered harshly, and he heard the fear in the tremble of her voice. "Alika. Are you hit?"

"No. Don't let that dog move," Alika said. "This glass is going to shred her paws."

"I know."

"I'm covered in glass and barefoot, so I'm not moving either," he whispered back. "What the hell is going on?"

"I think I should probably be in the Witness Protection Program right now. This could be related to my current case," Sophie whispered. "We're pinned down, but at least they can't see where to shoot us with the lights off. I have to make a call." He heard beeping as she used her phone. Ginger whined.

Alika shook out his arms and hair gently. Shards tinkled as they hit the floor. He didn't want to give the shooter a target, or cut himself on the fragments of broken window, so he focused on getting clear of the glass.

Sophie whispered fiercely into the phone, but he couldn't hear what she was saying.

Below them, on the ground, lights bloomed on. Voices were raised from the surrounding small houses and semi-permanent tents Alika had glimpsed on his way up. "You okay up there?" A strong, feminine voice called from below.

"Yes. But the window broke, and there's glass everywhere," Sophie called back. "I'm calling the police. Someone shot at us."

"What? No way!"

Sophie ignored the semi-hysterical inquiries shouted from below and addressed Alika. "I think the shooter's gone. But we need to get out of here." Sophie flicked on her phone flashlight and shone it over the floor, assessing the damage. "I got ahold of my contact at the U.S. Marshals Service. She's going to talk to her superiors. In the meantime, I need to clear out and go dark."

"You can come to my hotel," Alika said. "Can you throw me my slippers? They're by the door." Alika caught the rubber sandals Sophie tossed him from where he'd left them beside the front door, Hawaii style. "I'm guessing 'going dark' means more than turning off the lights."

"You should go back to your hotel. And if that offer still stands to join you...I'll take it. I need to pack up and leave here permanently. It won't take long."

Alika's blood thickened at the thought of Sophie in his hotel room. *In his bed.* "Sure. Anything I can do."

He slid the simple shoes on and stood carefully, shaking the remaining slivers out of his clothes. "Let me take Ginger. I can wash the glass out of her coat and keep her out of the way while you do what you need to do to get out of here. I'm sorry, Sophie. This sucks. I know you liked this place."

"I did like it here. But I like being alive better, and they know where I am, now." Her body was a tense silhouette lit dimly by the flashlight. "I'll go to the ground with you. I need to talk to my land-lady." Sophie loaded Ginger into the dumbwaiter and lowered the dog as Alika headed down the ladder that led to the ground.

The woman who owned the place was a tall, rangy woman with thick braids and a no-nonsense manner. "Are the cops on the way?"

"I think Sophie called them," Alika said, unloading Ginger at the base of the tree. He caught the excited dog by her collar before she could run away.

"I did not call the police yet." Sophie was descending the ladder. "I wanted to talk with you first. I know you have illegals out here."

"You need to leave, Sophie, if you're into something bad. But don't call the cops, please."

Alika scowled. *They'd been shot at, and this woman didn't want them calling the police?* But this was Sophie's business. He was just a bystander, and he wouldn't second-guess her in front of a stranger.

Alika left the two women talking and led Ginger to the pickup truck he'd rented. The truck's bed was still piled high with expensive hardwood he'd bought that day.

Something smelled about the situation, but Sophie would handle it.

CHAPTER TWELVE

Sᴏᴘʜɪᴇ sᴡᴇᴘᴛ the glass out of the way with a little plastic broom, heading to the ladder leading to her sleeping quarters. With the point of her knife, she dug out the two slugs buried in the wall and dropped them in her pocket. *Never know when you'll need evidence of an attempted murder.*

She felt frozen, her emotions locked away in a case where they could be taken out and examined at some other time, when she was safe.

When Ginger was safe.

When Alika was safe.

Her heart did a little, involuntary flip remembering the moment of seeing Alika look down at his shattered beer bottle, astonishment and confusion on his face. Thankfully, her reflexes had taken over and she'd knocked him out of the line of fire.

She'd thought he'd been shot.

A call to the police was not something Rhonda the landlady would welcome, and the attention it would attract wasn't something she wanted to deal with, either. But Sophie would have to leave the property because of this incident. Rhonda was an illegal pot grower, and sheltered undocumented foreign workers on the property. "I'm following my conscience. This is a modern underground railroad," the landlady had told her.

Thankfully, Alika hadn't insisted on calling the police and was going along with the plan so far. She had reached Matsue on the phone and told the marshal about the attack. Matsue had directed her to disappear in the short term as best she could. She would contact her superiors about bringing Sophie into WITSEC until the Chang trial was over.

Slipping into Alika's hotel room under his registered name for the night was as good a way to hide as she could come up with on short notice. She was grateful he'd offered.

*Hopefully, he had two beds in the room...*she refused to let that thought go any further.

Sophie pulled up the floorboard and removed her small backpack of highly confidential items. She took out a plain black wallet containing cash, a credit card, and a Hawaii driver's license for her Sandy Mason identity. She put her Sophie Ang wallet into the pack, and replaced the floorboard.

She unplugged her laptop from the desk area. After that, it took her only ten minutes to pack the essentials that she would need, wedging clothing and bedding into the large hiking pack she had arrived on the island with. Anything else was merely extraneous fluff she'd used to pad this sweet little temporary nest.

Sophie hurried back down the ladder after sending the backpack to the ground via the dumbwaiter. She hugged Rhonda briefly and handed her a wad of cash. "You don't know who I am, nor where I went. Just my first name, which is Sandy."

The woman's sharp brown eyes moved over Sophie's face. "And that's nothing more than the truth. I don't know who you are. Or where you went. Or why someone's trying to shoot you. But you aren't the first such person I have sheltered here. Far as I'm concerned, you rented the tree house for a few weeks and disappeared, after breaking my window."

"Perfect."

"Good luck. Stay safe." The woman hugged Sophie briefly.

Sophie was grateful for the moment of human contact as she hurried into the dark, heading for the Jeep. She removed a flashlight and an explosives detection wand out of her small pack and took a moment to check the vehicle over thoroughly for signs of tampering, grateful for the training and tech skills she had gained to monitor for such concerns.

Alika's confused expression as he looked at the shattered beer bottle in his hand filled Sophie's mind's eye once again as she started the Jeep.

Alika was a civilian.

He had physical skills and good instincts. He was strong, smart, and good with people. But he wasn't ex-Special Forces like Jake, equipped with training and the background to handle the situations that Sophie repeatedly found herself in.

This was a good part of why they had broken up the first time. Her life was dangerous. Alika could be used as leverage against her, even become collateral damage. She'd hoped things would improve with Assan Ang's death, but this new situation was just as potentially deadly.

She was going to have to go off the grid again, assuming her Sandy Mason identity, or go into Witness Protection. Either way, she couldn't endanger Alika by being involved with him until the Chang threat was dealt with and the trial was over.

And that could take a while.

Sophie's hands opened and closed on the steering wheel as she drove to Hilo Bay, taking winding side roads and watching her mirror constantly. She pulled off the road at one point and hid among some parked cars, checking for a tail. When she arrived at the Hilo Bay Hilton, she was sure she hadn't been followed. She parked in the hotel's garage and texted Alika.

"I'm here. Where's Ginger? I'm sure they won't let her up inside the hotel."

"She's settled for the night in my truck. Lots of water, and a nice

beach towel to sleep on. She will be fine. Parking spot B-17 if you want to check on her. My room is 307."

Sophie locked the Jeep and went to check on Ginger.

The Lab lunged to her feet when Sophie tapped on the window. Alika had left the windows cracked, and a large dish of water rested on the floorboard. She stroked Ginger through the window with the tips of her fingers and felt the dog's damp coat. Alika had found a way to wash the glass out of Ginger's fur, just like he said he would. Her heart swelled painfully at his thoughtfulness and support in this latest fiasco. "I'll see you in the morning, girl."

ALIKA'S ROOM overlooked Hilo Bay with a lovely balcony, the sliders open to a warm night breeze that stirred the curtains. Shades of cream and blue, and casual rattan furniture invited Sophie to drop her heavy pack and lean it against the love seat of the lounge area in front of the sliders. Two comfortable-looking chairs framed a television and coffee table.

Sophie's heart felt heavy as lead. She was saying goodbye to Alika tonight, for who knew how long—and she'd have to lie to him. He'd never accept that she was cutting him off for his own protection.

But no. She couldn't lie to him. He knew her too well, and she just wasn't good at it.

"What will you have to drink?" Alika stood at the small wet bar, rattling bottles.

"Whatever you're having." Sophie peeked into the adjacent bedroom. Oh no. *One king size bed.*

The depression's gray draperies fluttered at the edges of her consciousness, eager to drag her down into familiar blackness. *But she couldn't give in.* She had too much to do, and no safe haven to hide in while the darkness engulfed her.

Alika held out a drink in a clear plastic cup. "Here. Medicinal purposes."

Jake had said the same thing to her, not long ago. Sophie's heart gave a painful squeeze. This whole situation had to end, and it was going to. She took the liquid and threw it back in one gulp.

A rocket of heat burned down her throat and detonated in her stomach.

Sophie bent at the waist, gagging and gasping. Alika thumped her on the back and took the empty cup out of her trembling hand. "Not meant to be hammered like that, girlfriend."

"I'm not...your girlfriend." Sophie mopped at streaming eyes.

"Just a manner of speech. Obviously." His voice was tight.

"What was that?" She coughed.

"Vodka. Neat. You said to give you what I was having." He returned to the bar and cracked another tiny bottle, dumping it into the cup. "Go slow next time. Here's to surviving a shooting."

Sophie took the plastic cup and clinked it against his. She sipped this time, but it didn't taste any better. She grimaced. "I dislike this drink."

He cocked his head. "What do you like?"

"Sweet drinks. Amaretto. Blue Hawaiians."

Jake knew what she liked to drink. He'd studied her like a topographical map. He'd handled her like one, too.

Why was she thinking so much about Jake?

Because she'd been with him recently, and because she wanted to sleep with Alika now. The recent trauma of their attack still vibrated along Sophie's nerve endings, generating an elemental need to feel alive...and push back the darkness of her depression for just a little longer. *But that wasn't all it was.*

Her gaze followed Alika's graceful movements as he walked across the room and onto the moonlit balcony. "Come out and see the view."

Alika was daring her to recreate the dangerous situation they'd just been in; he was showing her he wasn't afraid. *But what if they'd been tracked?*

"No. Come in here, please. I can't guarantee it's safe. For either of us." Sophie's voice trembled. "I care about you, Alika, and what happened at the tree house was way too close for comfort."

He came back inside. Shut the slider and locked it. Slid the drapes shut. The room was lit solely by one corner lamp.

Alika stood in front of her. She stared at the art on the wall, avoiding his eyes.

"You seem...off. Are you okay? Having delayed shock?"

Sophie finally looked straight ahead, at the divot between Alika's collarbones, at his wide, strong throat. He was wearing a white hotel bathrobe, open to the chest. The smell of soap and clean male filled her nostrils. His buttery-brown flesh reminded her of satiny water sliding over smooth, hard river rocks. Her palms itched, longing to touch him.

They stood there for a long time, but somehow it wasn't awkward. Finally, she set a hand on his chest. His heart hammered beneath it.

"I'm thinking of having sex with you," she said. "Goodbye sex."

Alika took the empty plastic cup from the nerveless fingers of her other, dangling hand, and set on the bar. "Why goodbye?" He was in her space, this time drawing her close, folding her into himself. She shut her eyes and breathed him in. Her cheek rested on the warm skin of his neck. His voice vibrated against her lips. "Because I'd call it long overdue."

His strength surrounded, upheld, and enfolded her. Her eyes fluttered shut as his hands wandered.

She had to be honest. He had to know what he was getting into. She forced the words out. "I have to go tomorrow. Disappear. I can't see you any more until this case is over. My life is too dangerous for you..."

"I don't care about any of that. I love you." His voice was rough, his touch possessive. Alika tipped her chin up and kissed her, tilting her head so he could taste her deeply.

She closed her eyes and surrendered to the wonderful feelings he stirred in her body, in her soul. *He'd always made her feel so good.* This was not a crazy passion; this was a deep one, stoked by years of knowing, waiting, wanting.

She was hardly aware of moving into the bedroom, of undressing, of anything but his confident, loving touch, rich smell, delicious taste, the murmur of his voice whispering "I love you. I love you."

And then the world shrank down to nothing but skin against skin, muscle against bone, heart against heart.

Maybe now would last forever, tomorrow would never come, and she'd never have to say goodbye.

Another part of her knew better. Despair made her weep with more than passion at the end.

CHAPTER THIRTEEN

ALIKA REACHED FOR SOPHIE, his arm sliding across the silky bedclothes.

His hand came up empty. That sensation brought him into full awareness.

The room was dark, the curtains drawn as he remembered doing during an evening that seemed like a long time ago. The faintest glow of dawn outlined the sliding glass door's shape.

She was gone.

He rolled out of bed naked. "Sophie?"

Silence and a sense of emptiness. The sheets were cold on her side.

She wasn't just gone, she was long gone.

But he searched anyway: in the bathroom, in the living area. Every trace that she had ever been there was gone, except for a note on the hotel stationery in her elegant, back-slanted, Cyrillic-looking writing, left on the bar and held down by one of the small, empty liquor bottles.

"I thought it might be easier to say goodbye this way. I have to stay far away from you, for your own safety. Please don't look for

me, because you won't find me. I had to take your keys to get Ginger out of your truck. You will find them at the front desk."

No signature.

No "I love you," to match his own stupid declarations.

No promises of any kind. She hadn't even left him her name.

Just goodbye. *"For your own safety."*

Like he was a child in need of protection.

He was a trained fighter. Talk about hitting a guy where it hurts.

Alika staggered, off-balance with the pain, into the little kitchen area. He cursed, but nothing was big enough, bad enough, to express the feeling pulsing through him. The angst he'd felt outside the restaurant was just a shadow of this body blow.

She'd told him it was goodbye. He remembered her rush of words. It hadn't mattered in that moment.

It sure as hell did now.

He'd been in love with her before...but now that he'd had her body, all he could think of was the next fix he could get of her presence. Like a drug addict craving a high, need for her crawled along his nerves, consumed his mind, crippled his objectivity.

"This is the worst," he muttered. All the ridiculous love songs he'd never understood suddenly made sense.

She had made coffee. An inch of liquid was left in the little carafe when he picked it up. It was cold—that's how long she had been gone.

Still holding the coffee pot, Alika went to his pants, dug out his phone, speed dialed her mobile.

"This number is no longer in service."

He couldn't even leave her a voice message bitching her out for treating him this way. *Sophie was gone.* The feel of her was still impressed on his body, the smell of her, the taste of her. "Damn it to hell."

His arm twitched with the need to throw the glass container, to hear it shatter, to wreak some freakin' mayhem on something.

But what would a temper tantrum accomplish? It would only prove that he was the child she thought he was.

Sophie was wrong. He could manage himself, and even make himself useful. He thought he'd proved that on Kaua`i when they'd rescued a boy together.

Alika set the carafe down very deliberately, as gently as his desire was to break it. He walked to the drapes and pulled them open. He stood on the little deck to greet the new day, looking out at the sun just striking the water of Hilo Bay.

Sophie thought she knew him. She'd decided their lovemaking was just a goodbye screw, when to him it was the culmination of years of longing and desire, indescribably meaningful.

She thought he was *afraid* of the demons she was facing, that he couldn't deal with her problems. But she didn't know exactly what he'd had to do to get where he was, physically and emotionally.

And he wasn't giving up on her, no matter how she'd tried to ghost him: *because she felt something for him too.* Her body couldn't lie to him—he knew it like he knew his own. Her tears at that moment of completion were burned onto his skin.

He would offer her something different from the life she was in.

Kaua`i could be so good. They'd live in one of his houses. She'd do her investigation work and come home to him on the weekends. They'd train together, maybe coach people at their own studio. They'd have a couple of kids running around, room for Ginger and more pets. They'd be surrounded by *ohana*, and have a beautiful life.

Maybe she needed to know that was where he wanted things to end up.

She could disappear for now, but he would be waiting for her on the other side of whatever this latest thing was.

CHAPTER FOURTEEN

SOPHIE SLID into the booth of a Denny's on the outskirts of Hilo. Hazel Matsue sat across from her, already perusing a menu. The woman wore a sleek Nike running hat, the narrow bill casting a shadow across her sharp features. Sophie wore a ball cap, too, but hers was a trucker style in red, black, green and yellow, with a marijuana leaf on the front.

"Nice disguise," Matsue's mouth twitched. "Very Rasta chic."

Sophie plucked at her frayed black tank top. "I've been Sandy Mason before. She blends with some of the young local population here."

"And that's why I said nice disguise."

The waitress arrived. "I'll have coffee." Sophie usually drank tea, but today she needed something stronger. The single cup of weak brew that she had made in Alika's hotel room at three a.m. had done little but aggravate her sour stomach. Sophie extended the thick china mug, and the waitress filled it from a steel pot.

"Rough night, hon?" The waitress winked. "You look like you were rode hard and put away wet."

A sexualized colloquialism? Sophie kept encountering them. She wrestled her mind away from those hours in bed with Alika. She converted her British accent into something vaguely Australian and smiled. "Lots of good parties around here."

They placed their orders, and the waitress sauntered away.

Matsue leaned forward on her elbows as she perused Sophie. "You don't look like you slept at all last night."

She hadn't.

Sublime lovemaking had been followed by lying in Alika's arms as he slept, wallowing in guilt, regret, and depression. Negative emotions had kept her awake until she'd given up and sneaked out.

"Getting shot at by a sniper and having to abandon your residence will do that." Sophie sipped the coffee, disliking the bitter taste. "What did your superiors say about bringing me into the program? I thought I could just stay with you and Rayme. I could help with her security, since I'm already supposed to be doing that by private contract."

Matsue gave a brief nod. "I'm willing to bring you to the safe house, given what happened. It's an okay place to start, though I haven't heard back yet. Bringing you into the program is a process. Frankly, we don't have any information that shows this shooter was after you because of the Chang case."

Sophie's brows lifted. "What other reason would there be?"

"Some other case of yours?" Matsue sighed. "I don't know. Frankly, I think it's bullshit. But they don't seem to want to bring you in. I'm arguing for just a cooldown period; take you out of the mix for a while, and then have you go to another island or something. Lay low until the trial."

Sophie tightened her mouth. "I have a job to do, and I want to do it. I can help with Rayme, and, for once, she can help me, too."

"That's why I plan to take you out to the safe house from here. But you have to get rid of that Jeep, shed every trace of the life you were building here."

"I have some people I still have to see in Hilo tomorrow, but I can come out today." Sophie was in the middle of counseling with police psychologist Dr. Wilson. Her next appointment was scheduled for tomorrow afternoon.

And then, there was her father and Agent Ellie Smith. She'd texted the newest burner phone number to them, and they were expecting to meet her at a hotel in Hilo. "As to disassembling my life, I already did." Sophie had returned the Jeep to the rental agency. She'd taken a cab across town and rented a different car, using cash, from a cheap used vehicle place. The rusty blue Ford truck decorated with *Keep Hawaii Hawaiian* stickers was just the kind of car her character Sandy Mason would drive. "I already have a new burner phone. My Sophie Ang identity is retired, for the moment."

"You *are* a pro," Matsue said approvingly.

Their breakfast arrived. Sophie dug into the western omelet, surprised to feel so hungry; but that reminded her why. She wouldn't think of all of the activity of the night before.

She wouldn't think of Alika.

Wouldn't wonder how he would feel when he found her gone.

Refused to imagine him picking up and reading her note, trying to call her and finding her phone disconnected.

She had to be hard and cold and just walk away.

Her memories of Alika beaten, broken and in a coma could never be erased. That terrible incident on Oahu had happened to him because of her, and she wouldn't see him hurt again.

She'd warned him. She'd told him that she was going to disappear.

And he'd said that he didn't care, and that he loved her.

Bile surged up Sophie's throat in a burning wave. She gulped it down with the awful coffee, surprised to find that she'd eaten her entire omelet. She glanced at Matsue, who was working her phone and had hardly touched her breakfast.

"Let's just go out to the safe house, if you please. I need to get some rest." Sophie dug a twenty out of her mini-pack, laying it on the table.

"All right. We'll travel separately so we're less easy to spot."

Matsue forwarded directions to Sophie's phone. "I'll follow you, and make sure we are not followed out there."

"I know how to dodge a tail."

"Doesn't matter if you do or not. This is my circus, and these are my monkeys. And now you are one of them." Matsue met Sophie's gaze and smiled. She tweaked the brim of Sophie's ball cap with a compassionate gesture. "It's going to be okay, Sandy Mason."

Sophie took precautions driving to the safe house but never spotted a tail, nor even Matsue's vehicle, a nondescript beige SUV.

She turned off the main road and proceeded down a winding driveway. She pulled the Ford up to a metal gate. A simple wood frame dwelling on stilts with an open garage area underneath stood in the center of a neatly mowed yard on the other side of the barrier. All of the house's shades were drawn.

Sophie studied the simple metal fence and noted a telltale electronic wire around the top. Flood lights were mounted on all four corners of the house.

The place was secure and defensible, but to the casual eye, it looked like one of thousands of mostly empty vacation homes that took up space in Hawaii.

Five minutes later, Matsue drove up behind her in her SUV. She got out and unlocked the gate. "You wouldn't want to touch this fence," she told Sophie as she passed her.

"I noticed the electric wire."

"There are motion sensors, too."

Sophie drove through and parked under the house. She waited for Matsue to relock the gate before exiting her vehicle. Matsue pulled in and parked beside Sophie.

A door opened at the top of a flight of stairs going up from the garage to the deck as the women got out of their vehicles.

Holly Rayme peered down at them. She had color in her cheeks, and her hair looked washed and brushed. Her appearance was a big improvement over the last time Sophie had seen her. "Please tell me you brought something to eat."

"This isn't a restaurant, Ms. Rayme." Matsue sounded like they'd had this discussion before. "The cupboards are loaded with nutritionally sound meals, and so is the freezer."

"But I need fresh, organic food in order to support my recovery," Rayme whined.

Matsue tightened her lips in annoyance and gestured to Sophie. "Follow me."

The women ascended to the living area, which was as utilitarian and functional as it had appeared from outside. Sophie's gaze darted around, checking the security measures. The doors had extra reinforcement with metal backing and heavy gauge locks. The windows were small and high, letting in light but not allowing visibility into the building. Two bedrooms completed the floor plan, one with a queen size bed, and one with a pair of bunks.

Sophie turned to Matsue, her eyes wide. "These are the accommodations?"

"Yes. Best we could do."

"She's staying with us?" Rayme's voice rose to a squeak that grated on Sophie's nerves. "I don't want to share a room with her!"

"Ms. Rayme, if you don't stop complaining I might have to kill you myself." Matsue's voice was matter of fact.

"This sucks!" Rayme slammed the door and withdrew into the bedroom with the two bunks. The television Sophie had spotted in the corner of the room blared on.

"Thank God for Netflix," Matsue said. "They say drug addiction arrests emotional development, and I believe it. Holly is thirty going on twelve."

Sophie propped her large backpack against the couch and sat down at the kitchen table. She shook her head. "I'm not sure I can be that woman's roommate."

"Well, if you have a better idea, I'm all ears. But I'm not giving up my room. They don't pay me enough as it is."

"I do have a better idea. Why don't I set up a tent for me and

Ginger out in the yard? We can have a measure of privacy, at least for sleeping, and still benefit from the security of this location."

"That sounds okay, though obviously a tent isn't much shelter from a bullet."

"I'll set it up under the house. We can park the vehicles to provide cover."

"Worth a try," Matsue said. "The risk is on you."

Sophie unslung the small rucksack holding her laptop and personal items. Ginger, after nosing around, settled at her feet. "How is your Wi-Fi?"

"Not good, but we had fiber optic cable run to this house. I can give you a secure access code to go online," Matsue said.

Sophie located the cable hookup and plugged in her laptop. "I plan to keep helping with the investigation as we move forward. I have some information to share with you, but I have to run some analysis first."

She had decided to test Matsue's confidentiality before letting her know about the leak that Connor had located inside of WITSEC.

She would give Matsue a bit of false information and see what she did with it. If the woman passed it on, she was the mole they were looking for. If not, Sophie could bring Matsue into working on the leak with her and Connor. It would be invaluable to have an agent on their side who could share agency access from the inside out.

"Do you mind if I get started on pulling together some of the data I've been working on?"

"Of course, please do. I have to compose a report anyway about why I am bringing you onto the site." Matsue opened her laptop as Sophie took out the solid-state drive containing the Ghost's software.

She plugged it in, booted it up, and activated mirror VPNs to mask her location. The IP she was using was already secure, but with the leak they had, she couldn't be too careful. She sent a quick message to Connor: *"I'm in with WITSEC. Going to test the agent I'm with now. If she's good, we can bring her in to help."*

Sophie stared at the pulsing green cursor for a long moment, thinking. Finally, she typed, *"Do you know anything about the* Yām Khûmkạn*?"*

And then she shut down the chat window and removed the SSD. Matsue, on her side of the table, appeared oblivious, lost in her own work.

She booted up DAVID next and checked her caches, then she tossed out the bait. "I have intel through my data analysis program on a possible breach in WITSEC."

Matsue glanced up to meet Sophie's eyes, her brows drawing together in a frown. "How could you know anything about that?"

"Don't forget, I was the one to locate the 'Jones' family body dump. After that discovery, I put some online countermeasures to work, and I found a possible breach in your agency," Sophie said.

"When you lie, make it as close to the truth as possible," Connor had told her once. "That way you can speak with conviction." He would know. The Ghost was a master of misinformation.

Matsue looked over at Rayme's closed door. They could still hear the muffled dialogue of her TV program. "You have to share this evidence with me," Matsue hissed.

"You can't tell anyone," Sophie said. "Not even your supervisor. Until we can set up some way to stop the leak."

Matsue tightened her lips. "You're throwing around some pretty heavy accusations, and I don't even know you. Why should I believe anything you're saying is true?"

Sophie shrugged. "Suit yourself. But you must suspect something is wrong."

"That family had an identifiable security breach."

"And that's how your dirty agent is hiding the leak: by selling out only the info of witnesses who don't follow protocol exactly."

Matsue glared.

Sophie stared back coolly.

"All right, I'll bite. What's this breach?"

Sophie had already set up a hidden keylogger file with a link back to her cell phone that recorded everything Matsue typed. "I found a virus that's tracking your inputted case notes and is mining for witness locations." The truth was close.

"I have some skills. I can look at the data and see if it's what you say."

"But you can't report it to your superiors. We will monitor it instead, and let it lead us to the IP of the agent running it," Sophie said.

Matsue's mouth turned down. "That's not the protocol."

"But as an outsider, I don't trust anyone in your agency. And I don't have to. I'm choosing to trust you, only."

Matsue got up. She strode back and forth, a slender wand of coiled tension. Sophie tried to read if that strain was a dirty agent on the edge of discovery, or if her body language was that of a loyal one caught in a difficult situation.

She could not tell.

Truth was, Matsue's flat expression would have been hard for even Dr. Wilson to read.

"All right. Send the info to me," Matsue barked. "And tell me what we're going to do to stop this."

Sophie sent a screenshot of the code as Matsue sat down in front of her laptop. "I'm planting an additional bit of code that will mirror back to me what the virus does," Sophie said. "We can see who it's communicating with." This was a simplified explanation of what Connor had already set up online.

"I don't like it." Matsue stared at her computer screen.

Sophie met the woman's eyes over the top of her computer. "And you think I like being in WITSEC, knowing you have a leak in the program?"

CHAPTER FIFTEEN

PIM WAT SMOOTHED the turquoise cheongsam dress down her petite, delicately rounded body, pleased with the way the custom-fitted silk hugged her slender curves.

"You haven't aged a day, mistress," her maid cooed, tugging the hem, patting and smoothing the fabric over her hips and buttocks. Armita had been with Pim Wat since childhood and was allowed such liberties. The dress came to Pim Wat's knees, but a slit rode high on one of her slender thighs. Her legs looked endless in a pair of ankle-laced Louboutins. "No one would believe you were the mother of an almost thirty-year-old woman."

Pim Wat narrowed her eyes. "Stand, Armita."

Armita stood. Pim Wat's heels caused her to tower over the smaller woman. "Put out your arm."

Armita did so. The maid shivered with fear. *Good.* Fear was essential, as was the hope of praise, even for a servant as loyal and intimate as Armita.

Pim Wat dug her nails into the skin at the back of the woman's arm and twisted the tender flesh in a vicious pinch. Armita cried out but didn't move away. *She knew better.*

"Never speak of my daughter. You have lost that right. And never remind me of my age. I am ageless," Pim Wat hissed. "Say it. Feel it. Believe it."

"You are ageless, mistress, a goddess. Beautiful and eternal as dawn breaking over a new day." Armita's large brown eyes shone with conviction, with feverish passion. "I only meant to say so and was clumsy about it. Let me worship you."

Pim Wat considered. Armita was skillful with her hands, mouth, and a few key sex toys. It might be good to go into this meeting with the glow of an orgasm on her cheeks. Her eyes flicked to the clock on the wall of the luxurious suite. "No. There is no time."

Armita's gaze fell, her whole body slumping in disappointment. Pim Wat extended a finger, lifted her chin. "You still please me. You may worship me later. But never mention my daughter. You know why."

"Yes. Because I failed you, mistress." Armita's eyes stayed down. Her lush mouth drooped. "The kidnappers took Sophie Malee on my watch. I can never be forgiven."

"Exactly. But we can forget, for a little while." Pim Wat leaned in to kiss Armita's forehead gently. "Now get my purse. I want to go down early and get the right spot."

Pim Wat perched on one of the stools of the elegant bar at the Four Seasons Hualalai near Kona. She approved of the hotel's spare, modern, templelike ambiance with its terraced layout and emphasis on wood and glass. Sunset was just beginning to streak the ocean with gold and red, the colors of abundance and royalty.

She had seated herself in such a way that she could both watch the door and the view. The ocean, in the distance, was a restless cape of blue movement in the soft, warm evening.

The bartender handed her the martini she'd ordered. A nasty drink, but she liked the shape of the glass, the way her hand looked holding it. She sipped, and winced—the vodka burned, icy and tasteless.

Pim Wat spotted the CEO of Security Solutions as he stood in the bar's doorway, recognizing him from the bio picture on the company's website.

Sheldon Hamilton was well-groomed for a Hawaiian setting, wearing elegant clothing: a raw silk shirt, well-cut black trousers, Italian leather loafers. His dark hair was expensively barbered. Brown eyes behind stylish glasses scanned the room. He carried himself with the leashed power that spoke of a background in martial arts.

Hamilton had arrived early as well, no doubt hoping to have the surveillance advantage. Pim Wat's lips tightened in a tiny smile as his gaze flicked over her and moved on. She hadn't described herself; she had said only that she had an urgent need for his employee, Sophie Ang, and must discuss it in person. She'd had to bulldoze her way through several layers of underlings to get this meeting, and to judge from the man's tight jaw and tense posture, he wasn't happy to have been forced to come, even to a setting as beautiful as this one.

Pim Wat slid off the stool with a sinuous movement that rippled the tight silk dress, and that caught his attention—as did the slit to her thigh. She lifted her glass to identify herself as she caught his eye.

Hamilton's full attention felt like a heat-seeking missile headed her way. His focus raised goose bumps on her arms, tightening her nipples delightfully. Hostility radiated around him as he stalked through the bar—but by the time he reached her, he'd tamped it down.

The CEO stood before her, urbane and controlled, all that danger packed away neatly. "Madame Maison?"

"Oui." Pim Wat had adopted a French accent to go along with her favorite French identity. "So pleased you could make time for me." She extended her hand.

Hamilton took it, pressed it between both of his, holding her gaze with intense dark eyes. "Enchanté, Madame." He smelled delicious —some expensive, personally blended cologne. "I could not wait to meet this woman of mystery who is interested in one of my most valuable employees. And now, I'm delighted to have come all this way."

Pim Wat lowered her eyes modestly. "I hope it wasn't too far." She tingled, and wished she'd taken the time to get the edge off of her sexuality with Armita's help.

"Only a few thousand miles." Hamilton gestured to her glass. "I see you are already drinking. I'll have the same," he told the bartender. The man bustled off.

Hamilton gave Pim Wat a tiny boost onto her stool and sat beside her on his. She made sure her sleek bare leg was extended, brushing his trousers, and that their feet were aligned. Her sexy shoe looked perfect beside his equally fine footwear.

"I love the view here." Pim Wat's pulse fluttered. She savored the feeling. Almost nothing scared her any more, but something about this man both aroused and frightened her.

She ticked through the profile Armita had put together on Sheldon Hamilton: a reclusive billionaire computer genius, he was the head of a massive security company whose crown jewel was an artificial intelligence residential surveillance program. Hamilton had developed that program, along with his recently deceased partner, Todd Remarkian. Rumors persisted, but had never been proven, that the company had many shady clients on its roster.

Nothing about any of that explained the feeling Hamilton gave her, but Pim Wat had learned to trust her intuition. *There was more to this man than she yet knew.*

"I admit I'm jaded. I'm in a position to keep myself in beautiful settings as much as possible. This one is acceptable." Hamilton's teeth were brilliant as he smiled. "Tell me about yourself, beautiful lady."

"I am here on the island. Vacationing." Pim Wat shrugged. "I would like your employee, Sophie Ang, to do a computer-related job for me. I hope it wasn't too much of an imposition for you to meet me in person to discuss this. I left messages for Ms. Ang but she has not returned my calls."

"As I said, I almost never do client meetings in person, but this time, I'm glad I made an exception." Hamilton lifted her hand and played with her fingers, with the massive emerald that graced one of them. "How have you heard of Ms. Ang and her unique skills?"

"Oh, I have people who find me the very best things." Pim Wat smiled. "This emerald I'm wearing, for instance. It's called the *El Corazón de Colombia*. It's from the heart of one of Colombia's greatest mines. Flawless."

"It's exceptional." He continued to toy with the emerald, but his gaze was all on her. His attention warmed her like wax. "As are you, Madame Maison. Exceptional."

"Merci. You are too kind." Pim Wat blinked, breaking eye contact. She pulled herself together and took a sip of her martini. His drink had been delivered, and he clinked his glass to hers.

"To new partnerships."

"Yes. New partnerships," she echoed. *This man was getting to her!* She was supposed to be getting to *him*, finding out where her daughter was and leveraging her into the Yām Khûmkạn. "So, will you loan me Ms. Ang?"

Hamilton shook his head regretfully. "I cannot promise anything. She is an independent contractor, and right now, she's on an assignment. Unreachable. But if you are patient, I feel confident she will be interested in your opportunity." He sipped his drink. "Tell me more about it."

"Oh, I am disappointed. The situation is a bit time-sensitive." Pim Wat frowned. "Are you sure you can't...contact her for me? Put a word in her ear? It is a bit of foreign travel, but all expenses will be taken care of, of course."

"Of course. You were going to tell me more about the assignment?" His elegant brows raised.

He was hypnotizing her! The suggestiveness of Hamilton's voice, the cadence, the way he phrased things...thanks be to Buddha, she had been trained to recognize and resist hypnosis by the psy-ops arm of the Yām Khûmkạn.

"Oh. Yes." She sipped her drink. "It is a very sensitive situation. I have ties to the royal family of Thailand. My family assists with their security. Recently, there have been some...incursions." She might as well appear compliant, tell him as much as she could; there was no downside to that. "Our computer systems are outdated, but we are upgrading. We would like to install your artificial intelligence home security system in several very sensitive locations. Only Ms. Ang will be allowed to work in those areas. Because of her family connections."

"Tell me about her family connections." Hamilton leaned closer. His breath fanned her neck, her ear. His voice loosened her belly. She shut her eyes to fight the hypnosis.

"Ms. Ang is related to the royal family on her mother's side," Pim Wat whispered, allowing herself to bend in his direction, allowing her head to fall forward as if the weight of her long, thick, coiled hair weighed it down. "They will never trust an outsider."

"And you are close to them. To her."

"Yes."

"Sophie is a valuable asset to my company." His voice slid over her like satin fingers. The heat of his body was melting her clothing right off. "Will she be in danger?"

"Only if she betrays us," Pim Wat said. She jerked upright, blinking. She'd spoken too much truth that time.

He'd done it again! This man was dangerous.

She turned to Hamilton, sliding off the bar stool into his personal space, allowing her breast to brush his arm as she slid past him. "I must go. I will wait to hear from you. I trust it will not be long." She extended her hand for an obligatory goodbye, but barely allowed her fingertips to touch his, avoiding his eyes and his seductively murmured "au revoir, Madame."

She was desperate to get away, to shake off his spell.

Pim Wat walked stiffly, teetering on her heels, through the bar. She'd never been so clumsy in her life as she fought a magnetic pull to go back to him.

Pim Wat didn't breathe easy until she was on the elevator going back up to her room.

She had to stay far away from Sheldon Hamilton.

CHAPTER SIXTEEN

Sophie had arrived early for her meeting with her father and his Secret Service agent. She positioned herself behind a large potted palm so she could survey the Hilo Bay Hilton's busy foyer, and so far, hadn't spotted anyone who seemed to be tailing her. Because of her recent memories of this very place, she wished that her dad and Agent Ellie Smith had chosen a different hotel, but she had received a text that afternoon that they had arrived on island and wanted to see her right away.

Sophie's father, Francis Smithson, walked into the lobby with the ease of a much younger man, and Sophie felt a smile tug up the corners of her mouth as Frank opened his arms to her.

Her father was imposingly tall and broad-shouldered. His hair was going gracefully gray at the temples. His hug engulfed Sophie in warmth and support. "Even with all the mystery of why we're here on the Big Island, I'm glad of any excuse to see my girl."

Just the sound of Frank's deep, resonant voice could lower Sophie's blood pressure and make her feel happier, safer. She shut her eyes, leaning on her father's strength and breathing in his familiar spicy aftershave.

"I love you, Dad." They embraced for a moment, then Sophie

stood back. "Thanks for coming on such short notice. I'm sorry about the secrecy. When I explain why, though, you'll understand."

"I sure hope so. We had to do considerable rearranging to come over here." Ellie Smith's voice was mild as she walked up to them. The woman had intelligent deep blue eyes and wore her dark brown hair in a no-nonsense, sleek updo. Her crisp white shirt and navy trousers looked both stylish and functional. Sophie glimpsed the bulge of a sidearm under her jacket.

"Good to see you again, Ellie." Sophie shook the agent's hand. "I'm sure it was challenging to get Dad here. I wish I had a happier reason to see the two of you than what I'm going to tell you. We need to speak somewhere private."

Ellie nodded. "We'll go up to your father's room. I've already swept it for bugs."

On the ride up in the elevator, Sophie mentally ran through the story she would share. It wasn't going to be easy.

Her father reached out and tweaked off her ball cap, ruffling her short, dense curls. He tipped up her chin with a finger, frankly studying the scar of the skin graft running up Sophie's cheekbone and into her hairline as she gazed into his eyes. "You don't need to hide behind that hideous hat, Sophie. The scar gives you an air of dangerous beauty, of intrigue."

"Ha. Intrigue is right." Sophie's face was still a sore point for her. "I'm not hiding it, Dad. I'm undercover." She took the hat from his hand and put it back on.

Her father smiled. "I didn't think you were a huge proponent of the marijuana lifestyle."

Ellie Smith's expression was serious as she caught Sophie's eye. "Does this meeting have something to do with a case you're working?"

"No." Sophie pursed her lips. Smith wasn't acting too annoyed, considering the inconvenience and expense Sophie was putting them through—but Sophie couldn't discuss the Chang case.

The ambassador's hotel suite was the same layout and design as the one Sophie had just spent the night in with Alika. It was mildly tormenting to stand in an identical room, just a few floors above, and look out at the same view that she had experienced briefly for those blissful minutes.

"I need to make sure you're bug-free," Ellie said. Sophie extended her arms. Smith wanded her with a detection device, and nothing beeped.

"That's a relief. Glad I'm clear."

"Well, I would hope so. But you can't be too careful. In fact, since we were away, let me do the room again." Smith walked around and checked the room one more time. Finally, the agent drew the drapes so that no distance equipment could be employed to pick up the conversation.

"And to think these would have seemed like excessive precautions at one time," Frank said. "I know it's early, Sophie, but would you like something to drink?"

"Just a soda, Dad."

He brought her a carbonated beverage, and finally, the three of them sat in the living area.

"Some weeks ago, I was contacted by someone who asked me to meet at Hilo Bay Park. Said it was something to do with my mother." Sophie leaned forward, cupping the soft drink can in her hands.

"Your mother? What would there be to say about her? She's in that facility in Thailand." Frank frowned.

"That's exactly what I thought. In fact, if Auntie Malee had not kept me informed every six months or so, I would have no news of Mother at all. So, of course I was curious to see what this could be about, and who could possibly have the number for my latest burner phone. Fewer than ten people in the world would have the number." Sophie took a sip of her drink, her throat suddenly dry. "I went to the park with our dogs. Jake was with me at that time, and we had picked up a rescue dog. I ran the park with Ginger and Tank, and I tried to get a read on who it could be. Then, an old woman spoke to me from one of the benches." With an effort, Sophie kept her hand from trembling as she set down the soda can. "The woman was my mother, Pim Wat. She was in disguise."

"Unbelievable." Frank's eyebrows rose high on his broad brow. He uncoiled to his full height and stalked over to the bar. "I think I need another drink. Ellie?"

"No thank you. I'm still on the clock. Go on, Sophie." Unlike the two of them, Ellie Smith was perfectly calm, her legs crossed, swinging one of her gracefully shod feet. "I didn't know that your ex-wife…got out much, Ambassador."

"She doesn't. And that's why this is so astonishing. Over the years, Pim Wat has become more and more of a shut-in. She was institutionalized after a suicide attempt more than a year ago." Frank tossed back his drink. "I'm as surprised as Sophie must've been that she would make contact, and be physically present in the United States. Her depression is completely debilitating."

Her father was clearly every bit as deceived as Sophie had been about her mother's true level of functioning. There was comfort in that. "She looked exactly the same, Dad. I had not seen her in nine years, and she hadn't aged a day even though she was dressed as an old woman. She pulled it off perfectly. I completely failed to spot her." Now Sophie got up to pace. "She was neither friendly nor apologetic—none of the things I might have expected after such a long separation. She proposed that I join the Yām Khûmkạn, an ancient clandestine organization that guards the Thai royal family. She said my skills were needed to combat threats from cyber terrorists."

Frank swiveled to face Sophie fully. He stared in consternation. "I don't understand."

"Mother has been living a double life," Sophie said. "She isn't actually depressed."

Frank cursed. "Impossible."

"It sounds like your mother was attempting to recruit you," Ellie said.

"Exactly. Are you familiar with the Yām Khûmkạn?" Sophie asked.

"Yes. They are Thailand's equivalent of the CIA, or Israel's Mossad —but the organization is different in that it has been around for hundreds of years and is focused on the royal family, rather than serving the government in general. There is an almost religious, cult-like association within the organization. They have done an excellent job keeping a low profile, but we monitor them closely because aspects of what they do are like the Secret Service. They protect and guard Thailand's royal family, as you mentioned, as well as looking after their interpretation of the country's interests. But they don't answer to the regime currently in power, nor any political faction, which means they're basically a rogue group." Ellie accepted the soft drink Frank handed her and took a sip. "We also have reason to believe that the Yām Khûmkạn is behind several important international assassinations."

Frank was still shaking his head, the slow, dumbfounded movements of someone whose world has been rocked. "No. Not Pim Wat. She is...to put it kindly, a delicate flower. So easily stressed. Her depression was truly a disease. I saw it too clearly for it to be faked."

"Mother admitted that she really was ill at times, but not as debilitated as she pretended." Sophie rubbed her temples, her eyes closed as she recalled the painful, shocking conversation in the park. "She said she was chosen by the organization to marry you, Dad, so they could have intel on the United States. But Pim Wat was quote, 'not up to the task,' unquote. She told me that she should never have been a mother, that she wasn't up to that either."

"That bitch!" Frank said. "I should never have stayed with her as long as I did, but every time I tried to leave, she threatened suicide. Told me how terrible that would be for you."

"She blackmailed you, Dad. She blackmailed me, too, with the same thing." Sophie looked up into her father's devastated gaze.

He turned away to stare at the artwork on the wall, clearly unable to make eye contact any longer. "I'm sorry, Sophie. I had my work; I couldn't be there for you enough, but I stayed in the marriage until you were old enough to go away to school, where I hoped you'd get consistent care and exposure to the wider world. She wouldn't let me take you to the United States. Believe me, I just wanted to take you home." Her father's words came out in a rush, tumbling over each other, pressured by pain. "So now you're telling me that she was using me. Spying for the Yām Khûmkạn through my diplomatic position."

"Yes, Dad. That's why I asked for this meeting with you in person, and with Agent Smith as a witness. I don't want to be accused of being a security breach for even speaking with her. I knew how it could look, especially given the last couple of years in my personal life. That's why I'm throwing myself on your mercy, Ellie." Sophie turned to meet the woman's cool blue gaze. "Mother's tracked me down again since this first approach, via Security Solutions, and is asking for an answer. Rather than just shutting her down, I thought this might be an opportunity."

A long pause, as Ellie considered. "What kind of opportunity?"

"I could join the organization and feed you information from inside. Just as she did." Sophie was not sorry for the bitterness that colored her words. "It's even possible Mother still has some access to sensitive information through you, Dad. We need to identify any leaks and turn them against her."

"Why would she think she could make this appeal to you? Why would she think you would even consider it, when she has been such a poor parent?" Ellie cocked her head, inquiring.

"Because I always tried to do what she wanted. I tried to be a good daughter, so she could get well. She had much power over me in my early years." Sophie bit her tongue on sharing that her mother had virtually sold Sophie to her abusive ex, Assan Ang, in exchange for connections with the underworld in Hong Kong. Her father would be deeply hurt by that knowledge, and there was no point in doing that to him.

"Dammit to hell!" Frank was clearly struggling with his emotions as he strode back and forth. "I want to see her locked up. When I think of all the years I loved her, tried to help her...and she was just using me! Using *us*!"

There was nothing Sophie could say to make this any better. She had guessed how painful this might be for her father, akin to the shattering betrayal she herself had first experienced, driving her deep into the depression—all the way to a dark place where only Jake had been able to bring her back.

She shut down the memory of how he had done so.

"This is above my pay grade," Ellie said. "I have to get in touch with my supervisor, and likely, he will want you to talk to the CIA. If Pim Wat knows you've talked to your dad, all of our opportunities to manipulate her information stream will be lost. This opportunity will be lost. You have to string her along for the moment."

"I am not in a good position to be talking with anyone right now. I'm on leave from Witness Protection today to speak with you two," Sophie said.

"Well, when you can, I think you should contact her. Tell her you are angry about the personal failures between you. Try to get her to apologize. Make her wriggle on the hook a bit, to use a fishing metaphor. And when we have a solid plan, you can set up a meeting with her."

"*No!* Sophie has suffered enough! I won't allow it. I won't allow Sophie's life to be endangered, her emotions manipulated any more by that woman and her organization. Enough already!" Frank's face was dark with rage.

"Dad. I'm a grown woman. I make my own decisions," Sophie said calmly. "I can handle this. I've been through worse."

"And even that can be laid at your mother's door!" Frank stomped to the bedroom and went inside, slamming the connecting door shut.

Sophie met Ellie Smith's eyes. "I know how he feels. But he will eventually see that this is one of those times where one side of the coin is danger, and the other is opportunity. The best revenge I could get on my mother is to use her in the interests of my country."

"Thailand is also your country," Ellie said gently. "You have no loyalty to Thailand? To your Thai relatives?"

"I love Thailand. I do feel a connection to the place, the land, the culture. But I don't feel any connection to the royal family, the government, or even most of my relatives besides my Aunt Malee, my mother's younger sister." Sophie blew out a breath. "I was sent away to boarding school when I was twelve, and I never really returned. Maybe all of that was due to my mother's machinations. The United States has accepted me, nurtured me, given me a place to grow, thrive and belong."

"That's good enough for me, but it might not be good enough for the CIA," Ellie said drily. "Keep that burner phone charged, and in range. Where are you staying?"

"I cannot tell you that. I'm involved in a WITSEC case, as I said, guarding a witness at a secure location. But I will check in with you periodically, if I don't hear from you first. And I will reach out to my mother, as you suggest. Make her grovel a bit." Sophie's smile felt like a feral baring of teeth. "I will enjoy that."

"You deserve that, at least."

"I just hope Dad has someone to talk to about all this." Worry contracted Sophie's brow.

"He talks to me. We are friends. It will be all right." Ellie sounded absolutely confident.

Sophie nodded. *She had to hope that was true.* She left, shutting the door gently behind her and keeping the ugly ball cap pulled low as she exited the hotel room.

CHAPTER SEVENTEEN

Byron Chang laced his fingers over his belly and tipped back his chair. "So. You're telling me that you've made two attempts on those witnesses, and come up short?"

The assassin he'd had to hire, now that Akane was in prison, was a nondescript little Filipino man. The Lizard sported a tonsure of gray hair around a balding pate, wore horn-rimmed glasses, and he had a habit of stroking one hand over the other, as if handling a pet. The man appeared wiry and strong, though, and might have been younger than his current appearance. According to his dark net website, the Lizard was well-versed in disguise, spoke multiple languages, and could kill with any number of methods.

But he was damned expensive.

"I'm glad I only paid you half of your ridiculous fee," Byron said. "I'm beginning to wonder if you're the right man for the job."

The Lizard shifted in his chair, innocuous, but the narrowing of the man's mild brown eyes made the hair rise on the back of Byron's neck. "Both of your witnesses are in the U.S. Marshals Witness Protection Program now, which wasn't in our original contract and compounds the challenges. There's a back door into that organization, though, and I should be able to locate them and complete the contract within the week. I need more money to buy the information."

"You took this job as a bid. You have your first half. You should have budgeted accordingly. This is already triple what I usually pay for a hit." Byron missed Akane's skills more every week that went by with his brother in prison.

The little man flew around Byron's desk, knocked his chair backwards to the floor, and pressed Byron's own letter opener against his jugular so quickly that Byron hadn't even been able to follow the motion. "Do you want to live, Mr. Chang?"

The sibilant voice in his ear froze Byron even more than the sensation of a major artery throbbing against the razor-sharp point of the letter opener. "You'll never get away with killing me," Byron managed to rasp. "My people will find you."

The skin broke, and the burning sensation of blood welling made Byron's panicked heart race faster. He swallowed. The blade dug in deeper.

"Oh really?" The Lizard gave a humorless chuckle. "Do you think I don't know how to get out of this room and be long gone before anybody discovered your corpse? But then, I'd only have been paid half of what I am entitled to. And I have a one hundred percent track record for nailing my targets. I'm not about to ruin that for the likes of you. Unless, of course, you truly insist."

"All right, all right." Sweat beaded Byron's brow and burst out of his pores. "How much do you need?"

CHAPTER EIGHTEEN

Sᴏᴘʜɪᴇ ᴡᴏᴋᴇ ᴡɪᴛʜ ᴀ sᴛᴀʀᴛ. Black surrounded her. She blinked, but no light broke the seamless darkness.

She'd been so deeply asleep that she floundered for a moment, not sure which way was up, or even if she was still alive.

Her brain activated, providing necessary information: *she was lying on a relatively hard, flat surface.* There was soft, slippery fabric under her hands. She was warm and comfortable. Ginger was lying beside her, to judge by the doggy smell and faint, whuffling snores.

Sophie was inside the confines of her tent. Sound and light were filtered out by the closed door of the toolshed that the tent was pitched inside. The complete darkness reminded her of being in the lava tubes on Kaua`i.

Gradually, memory filled in.

She'd returned to the safe house after her meeting with her father and Ellie, carrying the gluten-free pizza Holly Rayme had begged for. The three women had eaten dinner together, but Sophie was battling the depression, and almost immediately, Rayme's complaining and negativity had driven her to seek some alternative to sharing a bedroom with the woman.

Matsue was uncomfortable with Sophie pitching her tent in the yard due to threat exposure. They had checked the built-in toolshed under the house, and other than a few rakes and a weed whacker, discovered that it was empty and just the right size for Sophie to set up her tent inside.

By then, the depression swamping Sophie was so powerful, its pull so strong, that she had hardly been able to muster the strength to put up the tent, unroll her sleeping bag, and crawl inside with Ginger.

Sophie registered the fullness of her bladder. The dog, sensing Sophie was awake, whined softly and nudged Sophie with her nose.

Ginger likely had to urinate as well. Sophie sat up, unzipped the tent, crawled out, opened the door of the shed, and let the dog out into the very early morning.

The last stars were fading from a deep cobalt sky just yellowing to the east, highlighted by the jagged silhouette of tree line encircling the property. Night-blooming jasmine planted in a clump nearby sweetened the dawn air. Coqui frogs filled the tropical air with their shrill, exotic song.

Sophie went up the wooden stairs into the house, stealing up the steps and unlocking the security measures with a set of keys Matsue had given her. She used the bathroom, brushed her teeth, and consulted her stomach. She'd barely managed to force down one slice of pizza last night.

As often was the case in her depressive cycles, she had no appetite. She drank a glass of water, however, knowing it was the right thing to do, and went back to her dim, cozy cave. Ginger met her at the door, and they withdrew into comforting darkness.

The next time Sophie woke, it was to the sound of pounding on the wooden door of the shed. "Sophie! Are you all right in there?"

Sophie forced her eyes open. She didn't want to let on how bad off she was—she was supposed to be helping with security. *She was supposed to be working.* But all the events of the last days seemed to have rolled down and landed on her like a boulder, flattening her under its weight.

"Yes. I am here. Just not feeling well."

Ginger backed that up with a loud woof.

"You've been sleeping all day. Do you need anything?" Matsue's voice sounded concerned.

"I am ill." There were many handy colloquialisms for this, but Sophie couldn't seem to muster one. Her brain felt like a wrung-out sponge.

"I have some leftover pizza we can heat, and a Skype meeting set up with my supervisor about bringing you into WITSEC. Are you well enough to join us?"

She had to get up for that, though the thought of more pizza made her stomach pitch. Sophie unzipped her sleeping bag. "I will do my best."

Half an hour later, Sophie and Matsue sat at the kitchen table with Matsue's laptop open to a secure video conferencing channel. The muffled blare of the TV in the next room testified to Holly Rayme's usual activity.

Sophie checked the artificial trace she'd attached to the screenshot she'd shown to Matsue. The trace had not been activated. *Matsue had not shared the intel with anyone.*

How long should she wait before bringing Matsue into greater confidence?

Maybe she didn't need to, until further down the road of working together. After all, the misinformation she'd given was truth, just not in the details. She would have to contact Connor and see how he thought they should proceed…

"Do you have any tea? Strong tea?" Sophie needed to be alert for this meeting, but getting to that state seemed impossible with the depression so heavy upon her.

"There are Lipton teabags in the cupboard." Matsue seemed frostier than her earlier demeanor. Sophie put the pot on for water.

Sophie had just sat down when a beep from the laptop informed them of an incoming call. Matsue answered it.

Matsue's supervisor was a trim man with round steel glasses, a military bearing, and silver hair. "Deputy Marshal Matsue. I understand you have another possible witness for us?"

"Yes sir. This is Sophie Ang. Sophie, meet Burt Felcher, Supervisory United States Marshal."

They nodded to each other, and Matsue continued. "Sophie is former FBI, and currently employed by a private agency, Security Solutions, to provide additional support on Holly Rayme's case. She is also the only other reliable witness against Akane Chang. As I told you on the phone, she had an attempt on her life via shooter just the other night, and she was also present during the attack at the jail. We have reason to believe that she is in just as much danger as Rayme, and I would like permission to officially enroll her in WITSEC. She can stay here at the safe house with our witness until the trial, and actually will be a big help in managing Rayme, who's a bit demanding."

"That sounds reasonable. I had a chance to run background on you, Ms. Ang, and you were quite the tech agent in the FBI."

"Indeed. That is true." Sophie did not want to discuss her past. "I would like to see this situation resolved as quickly as possible. Is there any chance the trial could be moved up, and the venue changed? I believe Rayme, and myself, are more at risk here on the Big Island where the Changs have so much influence."

"We are doing our best. The change of venue motion has been filed. We will keep you apprised. In the meantime, stay vigilant." Felcher signed off.

The women stared at each other. Matsue closed her laptop. "You don't look well."

"I don't feel well." Sophie stood. "I have a couple of phone calls to make, and then I'm going back to bed."

Rayme opened her door and peeked her head around the corner. "How much longer are we going to be trapped out here in the boondocks? I'm going crazy here with nothing to do but look at the two of you and Netflix."

Matsue rolled her eyes.

Sophie took that opportunity to fill her water bottle at the sink and go downstairs to her tent as the marshal argued with Rayme about a trip into town.

Sophie dug the bottle of antidepressant medication out of a pocket in her backpack. She had been missing doses, and that definitely wasn't helping her current state of mind. *There was too much going on for her to just sink into the pit and wallow!*

She tried to remember what the trigger had been for this latest episode, but her mind shied away. Getting shot at and losing the tree house? The meeting with her father and Ellie? Having to be stuck out here with Rayme and Matsue, with her life in danger?

No. None of that, while stressful, hollowed her belly and squeezed her chest like saying goodbye to Alika after their night together.

She'd tried so hard to forget, to minimize and ignore the wrench of that separation, but losing Alika was what was really getting her down. Her mind circled back and around, trying to find some other solution, but there was none. *Even when this current crisis was resolved, her lifestyle just wasn't compatible with his.*

Ginger trotted to the toolshed from exploring the yard and nudged Sophie with her nose. "Good girl. We should run, just because we should get exercise. But first I need to make a couple of calls."

Her voicemail light was blinking. Sophie saw messages from Jake, Marcella, and her father.

Sophie didn't listen to them, though; instead, she thumbed through her contacts to the number for Dr. Wilson. She called the psychologist and left a message canceling her appointment. "I'm sorry, Dr. Wilson, for the late notice, but I'm in a situation and can't continue with counseling for the time being. I will get in touch as soon as I am able." She ended the message with a press of the button on her phone.

Sophie tightened her jaw as resentment rose up. She'd been

trying so hard to have her own journey, her own experiences. Once again, her life was waylaid by a crime landing at her feet.

Dr. Wilson's question to her during one of their sessions bubbled up—*was some part of her wanting to solve crimes more than anything else?* If so, she was continuing to make her own destiny. She couldn't seem to turn away when cases came to her, and she was closing the door on anything but this dangerous choice of career.

Sophie tied on her shoes and, with Ginger at her side, ran around the yard, pausing to do sit-ups, burpees, and crunches until the tiredness she felt was that of the body, and not just the soul.

CHAPTER NINETEEN

BOREDOM, tension, and incompatibility with Holly Rayme made time in the next couple of days seem to slow, sand grains falling individually through an hourglass. Sophie battled her depression by running, working out with makeshift weights, sleeping, and working on her computer.

She called her father back—the Secret Service was talking to the CIA. They would get back to her when they had a plan.

She didn't return the call from Jake. She was too conflicted about him to deal with his intrusive concern. Instead, she texted him daily to keep him from being overly alarmed.

She wouldn't think about Alika—how his arms had been home, his touch a flame and a caress. How he must have felt, reading her note.

She was done with men. Really, this time.

Without being able to talk to Dr. Wilson, cut off and isolated, the depression deepened. Sophie decided to return Marcella Scott's call; she needed to talk to someone. Sophie hit Call Back as she sat outside her toolshed abode in the onset of evening, days into what she'd begun to think of as exile.

"Hey girl. Thought you'd dropped off the planet." Marcella's upbeat voice brought a frisson of energy to Sophie.

The women had become close during her years of working for the FBI, and Marcella was still an active agent in the Bureau.

Sophie cleared her throat—her voice felt scratchy and hoarse, unused. There wasn't much she had found to say to Matsue in the last few days, and even less to Rayme. "Is this a secure line, Marcella?"

"Does a penguin poop on ice? A bear shit in the woods? You're calling an FBI agent on her personal cell phone."

"I suppose." Sophie rubbed the scar on her cheekbone, running her fingertips along the numb-but-tingly ridge. "I'm in the Witness Protection Program. I'm supposed to have cut off all contacts with the outside world. But I'm going a little crazy here."

"Whoa! Back up the bus. What the hell is happening?"

"Remember that serial case I was on with Jake?" Sophie filled in her friend on the events leading to the arrest of Akane Chang.

In the house overhead, she could hear Matsue and Rayme arguing, and the clash of pots in the kitchen. Rayme seemed to be feeling better—but as she recovered strength and health, she had become more argumentative and belligerent. Sophie didn't envy Matsue her job. "The apparent result was that a sniper tried to take me out when Alika was visiting at my tree house. Agent Matsue agreed to take me into the program until the case was over."

Ginger put her big square head on Sophie's thigh, emitting a sigh, and she stroked the dog reflexively. *What would she do without her canine companion?* Ginger grounded her, got her out of bed each day and gave her a reason to run around the yard.

Ginger lifted her head, her floppy triangle ears pricked as she looked at the darkening jungle surrounding the square of open grass that marked the perimeter of the safe house.

"Holy crap. You should have called me! How long until the trial?" Marcella exclaimed.

"A month. I honestly don't know how I'm going to last out here.

The depression's bad, Marcella. And I...slept with Alika and said goodbye to him." Sophie's chest hurt with a pain she'd been trying to suppress. She pressed a fist against her heart.

"Geez! You needed that complication like a hole in the head, girl! What about Jake?"

"I told Alika about Jake. I told him I couldn't be in a relationship with anyone right now. But Alika...said he loved me. And we'd just been shot at, and I was hiding with him in his hotel room..."

"Oh my God. You and these men." Sophie could clearly see Marcella in her mind's eye, pinching the bridge of her nose in consternation. "Jake will shit a brick if he finds out!"

"I told Jake I wasn't with him. He understands."

"Right, he understands. He just doesn't know this happened. And no wonder Alika's been leaving me messages; he must be looking for you."

"Alika called you?" Sophie pressed harder against the thump her heart gave at that news. "He was almost taken out by the shooter who was going after me. After what happened to him before, I couldn't handle it if he got hurt because of me or one of my cases. He's a civilian. I'm a danger to him. I've totally cut him off. Changed my phone again, which I had to do anyway."

Sophie could practically hear Marcella thinking this over. Ginger put her head back down on Sophie's thigh.

"You're going to have to stick to your guns, Sophie, and resist temptation, because from what I can tell, Alika's not accepting good-bye," Marcella said. "But I think you're right to break it off with him entirely. Alika's a great guy. He's even got a lot of skills. But he's not trained like we are, like Jake is. He's not equipped to deal with your lifestyle."

Sophie hung her head, bowing around the pain. *Her friend agreed.* Alika needed to be kept far away from the train wreck that was Sophie Ang and her perilous, insane life.

"You should probably scrub Jake too, right now, if the Chang case is this hot," Marcella went on. "Those gangsters are ruthless. In fact, I hate to say it, but you should ditch this phone and not talk to any of us until the trial is over. Follow the WITSEC protocol. I want to see you alive at the end of all of this."

Sophie opened her mouth, then closed it again. She couldn't tell her friend about the WITSEC leak—that knowledge was too sensitive.

Ginger's head flew up and the dog lunged to her feet with a "woof!"

Overhead, Sophie heard the sound of shattering glass. "Gun!" Matsue bellowed. "Take cover!"

The lights went out upstairs as Ginger galloped away across the grass toward the darkening jungle, barking.

Sophie squelched an instant protective impulse to run after the Lab—the shooter was likely using a distance rifle. A moving dog wasn't going to be his main priority.

Sophie and Rayme were his main priority.

"What's going on?" Marcella's voice was a squawk coming from the phone Sophie barely remembered holding in her left hand as she drew her weapon, stashed in a cargo pocket, with her right. She scrambled backward, taking shelter behind one of the thick wood pillars holding up the house.

"We're under fire. I have to go." Sophie punched OFF and stashed the phone. "Are you all right up there?" She called upstairs.

"Rayme is down. I've called for backup," Matsue yelled. "I've cut the lights so he can't see us. Stay behind cover!"

"My dog…" Sophie's throat closed on the words as Ginger reached the perimeter fence and slammed into it. The Lab yelped and leapt back from the electric charge, then made do with barking furiously at whoever was on the other side. "Ginger!" Sophie called the dog. "Ginger, come!"

She ticked through her options, frantic to get Ginger out of harm's way.

The best thing she could do was to hold position out of the line of fire.

Finally Ginger broke away from the fence and trotted back, tail waving, clearly convinced she'd vanquished the danger.

If only that were the case.

The leak at WITSEC had caught up to them—and Sophie, with her trip to town to visit her father and Agent Smith, had provided the protocol violation the mole would use to hide selling out their location.

But had Sophie even been officially admitted as a witness when she made that trip?

Maybe the assassin hadn't come for Sophie, didn't know she was even there. Had only come for Rayme. But now, he knew Sophie was here as well because Ginger was her companion. Ginger made her a target.

Staying behind cover, Sophie dragged Ginger by her collar to the shed and shoved the dog inside, closing the door on her whimpering cries. "For your own safety, silly girl," Sophie scolded, and ducked around the shed, heading for the stairs.

A silenced bullet plowed into the wooden railing of the stairs beside Sophie with a *thwack,* spraying her arm with splinters. Sophie barely felt the sting as she hurtled up the stairs and dove into the house, slamming the door behind her and locking it.

"Son of a bitch." Matsue was directly in front of Sophie, kneeling beside Holly Rayme's prone body. "I guess that answers the question about whether or not the shooter is still around."

Sophie crouched beneath the level of the windows and joined Matsue. The exterior sensor lights had come on, and in the reflected glow coming through the windows, the deputy marshal held a bunched towel pressed against Rayme's chest. Blood soaked the white terrycloth Matsue held. The woman was ashen, her eyes closed, her breath a wet rattle. "She looks bad."

"She is bad. Ambulance is another ten minutes away." Matsue's phone was sandwiched between her ear and shoulder. "Hilo PD is on the way too."

"How did he get her?"

"Rayme opened the blackout blind over the kitchen sink, and that's all it took. He must have been watching us for a while."

Sophie glanced up at the broken window. Memory of her recent attack at the tree house surged back with way too much clarity.

"You're going to want to get that dealt with." Matsue gestured with her chin.

Sophie looked down. Several three-or-four-inch wooden splinters jutted from the meat of her bicep. As if in response to her visual survey, the area throbbed. Sophie reached up and grabbed a roll of paper towels off the sink. "I'll cover the door in case he tries to come in."

"Good idea. Though I'm betting he's done for the night. He likely knows we're armed and help is on the way," Matsue said.

Sophie carried the paper towel roll over near the door. She took up a position beside the aperture and set her weapon down on the floor. Using one of the paper towels, she gripped the heavy wooden splinters and yanked them out of her arm one by one.

"Gross, Sophie!" Matsue exclaimed. "I meant get medical attention, not do it yourself!"

"The splinters impair movement, and this is my shooting hand." As soon as the last one was out, Sophie's arm felt and moved better, though fresh blood welled from the puncture wounds. Sophie covered the site with a clean paper towel and pressed down with her left hand. She picked up her gun with her right hand, propping it on her knee.

The gurgle of Holly Rayme's breath slowed...and finally stopped.

CHAPTER TWENTY

HAZEL MATSUE DIDN'T SEEM willing to stop rendering first aid to Holly Rayme's body. She began mouth-to-mouth and chest compressions, muttering a count.

Sophie dragged a heavy armchair over against the door and rose to squat at the window facing the direction from which the shots had come.

Under the house, Ginger whimpered and scratched in the shed. The surrounding jungle wrapped around them in an impenetrable black silhouette, but Sophie could hear the slight susurration of wind in the trees, see the first stars piercing the bowl of Prussian blue sky, hear the frog chorus tuning up.

The tension, the waiting, reminded Sophie of a recent case she'd worked on Maui, watching for thieves who wanted to steal ancient Hawaiian artifacts.

She hadn't liked the tension and waiting then, either, but the stakes hadn't been this high.

Memories from that case flashed across her mind. She and Connor had been dating. Jake had been an attractive but complicated friend. Alika had been gone from her life at the time, fallout from an attack by her ex.

She should never have gotten involved with Alika—she'd just broken both of their hearts all over again.

What strange twists life could bring in just a few short weeks.

Sirens shredded the night with an unearthly wail at last. Organized chaos ensued, beginning with the harsh bark of Matsue's voice giving the gate code to the ambulance and backup units. Sophie put away her weapon, removed the barricade and unlocked the doors.

Holly Rayme could not be resuscitated.

Her body was checked over thoroughly as an exhausted-looking Matsue looked on. The time of death was pronounced, the body lifted onto a white plastic sheet, wrapped up securely, loaded onto a gurney, and strapped down.

Matsue met with the HPD detectives who had responded while the EMTs treated and wrapped up Sophie's arm. "These are deep," her medical attendant pronounced. "You should have a shot to prevent infection."

"I'm fine." Some strange mental concoction of shock, fatigue, and depression made her feel far away from anything with any meaning. Her arm scarcely seemed real.

Holly Rayme's body was driven away to the morgue. Sophie wished she felt something one way or another about the woman's death.

She was rolling up her bedding, stuffing it in the carrier bag, and wrapping bungee cords around the whole mess with Ginger looking on, when Matsue appeared at the door of the shed. "I have another location to take you to."

Sophie shook her head. "Obviously, the breach at WITSEC is a problem. I've lived under an alternative identity long enough that I can stay off the radar. I'll do better alone."

"I have a secure place. I won't tell anyone where it is, not even my next in command." Matsue's smooth brow was furrowed with stress. "I take this job seriously, Sophie. It kills me to lose a witness."

"I can tell. I saw you trying to keep Rayme alive." Sophie sat back on her heels. "But how long will they let you keep my location secret? I was thinking about how this hit unfolded, and I don't know if the shooter knew I was here until he spotted Ginger. Now he knows."

"About that. You need to find a place to stash that dog. She makes you recognizable. A target."

"I already thought of that." Sophie had come up with a plan for Ginger in the long minutes of waiting. Her father was still on the island at the hotel, waiting for the CIA's plan for dealing with Sophie's situation with her mother. She would give Ginger into Frank's care until after the trial. It hurt to even think about parting with the dog, but Ginger might have been killed this evening—and her presence made Sophie easily identifiable, no matter how she disguised herself.

Ginger, like Alika, was a liability.

"I have to give you my strongest warning. The Witness Protection Program is voluntary, but this is a bad idea. You're the only witness left that we can really count on. Whoever this shooter is, he seems to have both skills and knowledge." Matsue met Sophie's gaze with serious brown eyes. "Please don't go off alone. Let me help you."

"This is not your fault, Hazel." Sophie had never said Matsue's first name before, but it was past time. She respected the marshal. The challenge they'd shared of dealing with and protecting Rayme had brought them together in a silent bond. Sophie gestured to Matsue's white shirt, stained with Rayme's blood. "I know you'll do everything you can. But the deck is stacked against your agency right now with this leak we both know about. All it would take is one tiny mistake, like Rayme raising the blind, and if my location is known... I would be gone. I *know* I will be safer on my own. It's not a reflection on you. We can continue to work on exposing the traitor who's selling out Witness Protection." She hadn't spoken this much to Matsue in the days they'd spent together. Matsue handed her some of the tent's cords as Sophie went on. "I have an alternative identity. Two, in fact. I've done this before. Actually, I should never have come here. I worry that my trip to town to meet my father provided the security breach that the mole needed to release the information of this location to the killer."

"Sophie, no. That can't be the breach. You left here and went to town before you were even officially enrolled in the program."

"I also made a phone call or two."

"I just don't think that's it, Sophie. Don't do this."

Sophie shook her head and began disassembling the tent. "You said it. The Witness Protection Program is voluntary, and I am choosing to leave. Prepare any papers you need for my signature."

Matsue stared at her for a long moment, and then turned and walked away. Sophie heard the thump of her boots on the wooden treads of the stairs.

Sophie finished gathering her meager belongings and donned her backpack. She signed the release forms Matsue thrust at her. "Goodbye, Hazel. I'll be in touch when I can."

"Good luck, Sophie." Matsue tightened her lips. "You're making a mistake. But I'll be around if you need me, anyway."

"Thanks." Sophie tugged Ginger's leash and headed toward her rental. "See you at the trial."

CHAPTER TWENTY-ONE

A<small>LIKA STARED</small> down at the ring in his palm. The simple platinum setting flashed fire and rainbows from a row of large, channel-set diamonds. He pictured it on Sophie's hand. She had such beautiful, long fingers. She could wear a ring like this and make it look insignificant—and the setting was practical: there were no sharp edges or protrusions to catch on a weapon or her tech equipment.

"I'll take it."

"Oh, so pretty. Your fiancée, she one lucky lady," the sales-woman purred, slipping the ring into a little black velvet box, and then into a silken bag.

"She's not my fiancée yet." Alika felt queasy but determined. *"No way to know but to try. You give it your best, and leave God the rest."* His *tutu* Esther's voice filled his mind. She was a powerful *kumu* and elder, and her wisdom had often guided him.

"Well, she's lucky already, to have the chance to say no to a guy like you," the woman said. Alika glanced out the window of the store, uncomfortable. *There was a very good chance Sophie would say no.* "We don't take returns," the clerk went on, as if reading his mind. "But there's no way she will be anything but thrilled." The woman raked him with her eyes. "You're the full package."

"Not the right tone to take with me." Alika pulled the credit card slip over and signed it. "But thanks." He snatched the silky bag up and shoved it into his pocket, pushing out the door of the store onto the street.

Now all he had to do was find Sophie, and that was going to take some doing.

SOPHIE LAY on her back on the thin camping mattress that had become familiar in the days and weeks of her traveling, gazing up through the top of her pup tent. The rain fly was off, and she watched the interlaced branches of a towering old growth koa tree overhead through the screen. The gentle rustle of the wind in the branches filled the air, punctuated by the sweet song of native birds.

She could hear someone coming from a long way off through the delicate twigs and dry leaves that surrounded her campsite in a remote, overgrown *kipuka* in the wild expanse of lava between Hilo and Kona.

She closed her eyes and let herself relax. *No one could find her here.*

The last twenty-four hours had been a long, arduous blur, but Sophie finally felt safe and settled.

She had donned her outdoorsy Sandy Mason identity along with that woman's wardrobe of urban-hippie hiking clothes after dropping Ginger off with her father. She'd stocked up on supplies, returned the rental car and had taken a ride share to a popular trailhead off of Saddle Road. Saddle Road was a winding, two-lane thruway between Hilo and Kona, smoothed and tamed into a picturesque highway, upgraded from years ago when it had been a rugged four-wheel drive track.

Sophie had struck out across the raw lava with a compass and a good supply of water. When she found an isolated raised "island" of old growth forest in the plain of black lava flow, she'd set up her tent in a hidden grotto. Tree ferns surrounded her, their long ornate fronds bending to touch the ground, providing a screen for her camouflage-colored tent. Her campsite was just about invisible.

She was finally completely off the grid. She'd destroyed the SIM card of her latest phone, and hadn't given the number of the new one, still wrapped in plastic packaging, to anyone.

After recent events, being completely alone felt wonderful. The only one she missed was Ginger.

She soon fell asleep.

Sophie woke to a chill breeze rattling the tent and the tickle of rain on her face. She hurried out, putting up the rain fly just in time as the heavens released a deluge upon the area. She curled on her side in her sleeping bag and turned on her e-reader. She'd loaded the device up with books, and soon lost herself in a Steve Jobs biography.

Days passed. Sophie meditated. Did her yoga practice. Ate simple meals she prepared on her one-burner camp stove. She finished the Jobs biography, took notes on the character traits needed to be a leader, and started on the book Dr. Wilson had recommended to her, Mihaly Csikszentmihalyi's *Flow*.

She didn't sleep well at night. Memories of Assan's tortures assaulted her, along with doubts and self-recrimination about her current relationships and situation. She missed Alika and tried not to replay every moment of their night together, while also longing for the heat of Jake's solid body to keep her warm and pull her out of the deepening depression. Memories of recent ugly things she'd seen seemed to wait for night to bubble up out of her subconscious and fill her inner vision with nightmarish clarity.

The traumatic visions and mental replays increased and encroached onto daytime waking hours. She wandered the perimeter of the *kipuka*, staying hidden in the trees, feeling disembodied as she looked out over the empty, rugged lava plain.

She began to have trouble screening intrusive thoughts and memories out, even with exercise or reading.

Sophie lost track of the days. The depression became a constant sibilant whisper in her mind, sucking at her motivation to do anything but lie in her sleeping bag all day and stare at the trees overhead. She lost the energy to read, exercise, or care for herself.

She ran out of food, but it didn't matter because she wasn't hungry. And then, she ran out of water.

This did bother her. She felt weak and desperately thirsty. Dry mouth, cracked skin, and head and muscle aches assailed her.

Hunched in her sleeping bag, shaking with a low-grade fever, her lips painfully cracked, Sophie struggled to want to live. "I'm dying," she whispered, and realized it was true.

The depression had lured her out here into the wilderness, found a reason for her to cut off everyone who might be able to help her, and now it was going to kill her.

She didn't even need enemies like the Changs. She carried the most powerful enemy within herself, and no matter how she tried, the disease was always there, waiting to bring her down. "A sickness of the soul," her father had called it, and that, too, was true. *Another gift from her mother...*

Her mother, who had never loved her. Pim Wat had only used her, had given her this crippling illness, and now was back in her life to use her again.

She should just end the suffering quickly. Get the inevitable over with.

Sophie reached under the thin foam pillow and brought out her weapon.

Her hand shook as she put the black, boxy muzzle of the always-loaded Glock into her mouth. *One quick pull of the trigger, and it would all be over: no more pain of the mind, body or soul. No more conflict. Just peace...*

She shut her eyes. Her finger tightened.

CHAPTER TWENTY-TWO

PIM WAT PURSED her lips as she perused the vials in a small, locked metal box marked MEDICAL KIT. Each poison was labeled with an innocuous pharmaceutical name. Pim Wat checked the name against the code key she carried in her phone, touching each rare, valuable container. Handling the small glass bottles was soothing.

She'd received a text that there was a contract out on her daughter's life. She'd routed the text back to the Yām Khûmkạn, but their tech department was subpar without Sophie's skills to enhance it. They hadn't even been able to come up with a number for the phone that had issued the text, let alone an identity or location. She snorted with disgust, thinking about it.

The contract had been issued by the Changs, and it was related to the stupid case Sophie was mixed up in. There were a lot of moving parts, but Pim Wat had been able to verify that the contract was real.

She tapped her lips, considering. *Who should she go after first?* The issuer of the contract, the assassin, the leak in Witness Protection who had sold her daughter out, or the reason for the contract, Akane Chang?

She needed a lot more information to develop one of her Scripts.

She loved her Scripts: developing her role, her costume, the dialogue, the final scene. Even if her plays were never seen or known by anyone but those involved, she found satisfaction in deploying her unique talents in the service of her family and her country.

Armita was researching the likely players, but again—without good tech support and with few contacts in a foreign country, Pim Wat was operating in the dark in developing a proper Script and choosing a target.

The heat of rage flushed over her. *She wanted to kill them all.*

Pim Wat had not been a good spy, and she knew that. Her moodiness, low energy levels and impatience had made her information gathering skills less than stellar. But, it turned out, she had other abilities that the Yām Khûmkạn had been able to put to use. The elemental rage that lived inside her, tamped down and turned inward by her periodic depressive episodes, had found a useful outlet.

Perhaps she would get another text with more information. It would save a lot of guesswork and a lot of lives. It really didn't matter who was feeding her this information—their purposes were currently aligned. She would find out who it was eventually.

Pim Wat picked up the vial containing her favorite poison. Tasteless, odorless, clear as vodka, a microdot absorbed through the skin paralyzed the heart muscle in minutes and, to every examiner, appeared to be a heart attack from natural causes.

Pim Wat hadn't been able to help Sophie Malee when Assan had her—the Yām Khûmkạn had needed the alliance too much. But perhaps she could make up for it now. Killing all of them was not such a bad idea; perhaps it would purge the annoying sliver of maternal guilt that nagged at her whenever she thought of her daughter's suffering at that man's hands.

CHAPTER TWENTY-THREE

THE COLD STEEL banged against Sophie's teeth, sending a jangle of alarm through her body.

No. No. I don't want to die. I have fought so hard to live.

Her father Frank's face, crumpled with pain, rose in her memory. He wore an expression that had hurt her to see from her bedside when she'd been shot on one of her cases. He would suffer so much. She was selfish to even consider dying when she had a choice about it.

Other faces filled her mind, each of them grieving the news of her death.

Marcella. A friend who'd gone beyond the bounds of normal friendship many times, trying to bring Sophie back from the depression. She could picture Marcella, furious and grief-stricken, ranting at her gravesite. She could see Marcella kicking over the flower arrangements, bitching her out with curse words. The thought almost made her smile.

Dr. Wilson. The therapist would feel terrible. Wonder what she could have done to prevent this. Regret their missed appointments.

Lei. Her detective friend would weep for her, but she would find comfort in her husband and child. Lei was a painful source of envy and hope.

Alika. She could still see and feel his loving eyes and hands. "I love you, Sophie," rang in her ears. It was bad enough that she'd cut him off like he meant nothing to her...but *suicide?* He'd wonder what he'd done to contribute to her state of mind, and she couldn't deny that cutting him out of her life was part of her current hopelessness.

Jake. Jake would be crazed, might even hurt himself. She could see him lashing out at everything around him with the agony of a wounded animal, turning that destructive force on himself and others.

Connor. Connor would be the most lost and alone of all. She in all the world knew who he really was. He would blame himself. Who knew what darkness would be unleashed by his isolation and grief?

And Ginger. Even when Frank cared for her, the Lab lay watching the front door of the apartment, waiting for Sophie to return.

Tears tried to form in Sophie's dry eyes, burning them. Strangely, the thought of Ginger's grief moved her most of all.

Sophie took the gun out of her mouth and put it back under the pillow.

She crawled out of the sleeping bag, trembling with weakness even from that small effort, and made her way to the near-empty backpack. She opened the side pocket and dug out the plastic-enclosed phone.

She was too weak to get the heavy packaging open, and finally gave up.

The phone probably wouldn't work out here, anyway, and the battery wasn't charged. But her laptop might still work, and she had a satellite-enabled uplink. She hadn't turned it on in all the time she'd been out here.

She booted up the laptop. The battery was halfway charged. *Good. That ought to be enough.* She plugged in the Ghost software and sent a message to Connor with her GPS coordinates, and crawled back into her sleeping bag.

SOPHIE WOKE to the sound of her tent being unzipped. She reached under her pillow and drew the Glock, raising it in a shaky hand to point at the dark silhouette in the doorway of the tent.

"Sophie. My God." Connor's voice.

Somehow, crazy as it was, it was Jake she'd expected and hoped to see—but Connor was the one she'd been able to contact. *She shouldn't be disappointed.*

She lowered the weapon. "Connor. You got my message."

"I did. Seems it was just in time."

Sophie collapsed back into the foul nest of her sleeping bag, too weak and dehydrated even to speak. But it didn't matter, because Connor, being Connor, had brought help.

She was lifted by strong hands and loaded onto a stretcher. Murmuring voices. An IV was inserted into her arm. She faded in and out of consciousness as she was carried through the rough terrain of the *kipuka* toward a helicopter parked on the lava plain.

A helicopter. "Alika," she whispered, through dry, cracked lips, and felt a surge of something that might have been hope.

Connor was holding her hand, walking alongside two men bearing her stretcher. He squeezed it. "What? I missed that."

"Nothing." Sophie shut her eyes. *Alika wasn't piloting that chopper.* She was never going to see him again, and that was as it should be.

If she could have cried, she would have. *This was all wrong.*

Everything was loud and overwhelming, with a lot of jerking, bumping and swaying. She couldn't bring herself to care about any of it.

CHAPTER TWENTY-FOUR

THE NEXT TIME Sophie really woke up, she was lying on something incredibly soft and silky. Everything, including herself, smelled wonderful.

She opened her eyes.

A curved ceiling overhead. Recessed lights beaming down on her. Warmth. Classical music.

She was lying in a rather splendid bed in an oddly shaped room.

Sophie felt immensely better but had to pee. Urgently.

She sat up carefully, groaning at stiff muscles, and discovered she was still hooked up to an IV and a rolling pole was parked beside the bed.

Connor appeared in the doorway. "How are you feeling?"

She really looked at him for the first time. He was in his Sheldon Hamilton persona: dapper black trousers, an open-necked white linen shirt, those hipster black-framed glasses that hid dark eyes.

She hated his Hamilton persona.

"I am better, thanks to you, but I have to use the bathroom." Sophie swung her legs out of bed. She had been thoroughly cleaned and was wearing a set of white satin pajamas that might have been made for her.

Connor supported her by the elbow into a small, tidy bathroom. He shut the door, giving her some privacy, and Sophie sat on the steel toilet seat.

Immediate needs of nature taken care of, Sophie looked around. The wall curved here, too, and a small round window was double-paned.

All of the cues came together in a flash of insight: *she was on a private jet!*

Jake had said Sheldon Hamilton, CEO of Security Solutions, had a company plane. No wonder he had been able to reach her in time...

Sophie finished her business and washed her hands, avoiding looking at herself in the mirror. *Had he given her a bath while she was passed out?*

She rolled her IV pole out of the bedroom on trembling legs. Connor was seated directly ahead of her at a built-in dinette. A spread of amazing-looking food made her mouth water instantly.

"Did you give me a bath? Dress me in this?" She gestured to the satin pajamas.

His brows drew together. "No. I had a private medical service attend to you, the same one that was with me when you were found. You've been out for six hours since we got back to the plane and got you situated." Connor had removed the contacts that darkened his sea-blue eyes and the glasses that obscured them further, but she was still jarred by his dyed brown hair and reminded that he lived a double life. "You would have died in another day or two, the doctor said." His tone was carefully neutral.

Sophie had no response. She slid into the bench seat across from him.

Connor buttered a piece of flaky-looking croissant and held it out to her. "Don't eat too fast."

Sophie took the croissant and bit into it, closing her eyes to chew. The pastry melted in her mouth, and she moaned at the exquisite good taste. *How had she let herself get so far down that she almost did Chang's work for him?*

She let Connor feed her bits and pieces of eggs, fruit, and bacon, unable to even make the tiniest decisions about what to eat.

Her stomach rebelled, cramping painfully. She pushed the fork he held away. "Enough. Tell me what's been going on."

"A lot has changed since you disappeared." Connor set down the fork and sipped his coffee.

"How long has it been, exactly?" Sophie was sure of the first five days: that's when she had had food. It was the days after that that had begun to run into each other.

"It's been ten days since you left WITSEC. I don't know why you did that, by the way. I thought you were going to try to help me find the dirty agent from the inside." Connor was angry—she could read his bunched shoulders and tight jaw. "But you'll be glad to know that, in light of the main witness's death, the trial has been moved to Oahu. And it's only three weeks away."

Sophie didn't care, but she should. She struggled to find motivation to put her reasoning into words. "That is good news about the trial. And as to the other, I was pretty concerned about staying alive at the time I left WITSEC. I became ill out in the wilderness."

"Ill? Is that your euphemism, Sophie? Because it looks a lot like severe depression to me." Connor met her gaze with familiar eyes. "You forget. I know you very well."

"I am not well. You can call it depression if you like." There was no way to explain how she had allowed herself to get so close to death by dehydration—and her personal battle with her Glock would remain a secret. "How did you find me so quickly? I sent the message, but I thought you were out of the country."

"I had returned to Hawaii on some Security Solutions business, fortunately. It took a while to hire a helicopter and organize the medical team, and then find your location from the pingback. Are you feeling any...better?"

Connor was referring to her mental state.

Sophie's physical body was recovering rapidly. The other areas weren't worth discussing. She shrugged. "I reached out to you."

"Maybe you need more of a reason to live than just survival. Maybe you need to get interested in our case again. At this point, I am fairly sure you and I are the only way the mole inside WITSEC is going to be discovered and rooted out."

"Matsue knows about the leak now. She's interested in a positive outcome, especially now that her witness was killed. She seemed to take that very personally. As for me, I have to stay alive and testify at the trial. That is my sole priority." *If only the whole thing would just go away and leave her alone.* Sophie looked around the pristine interior of the jet, longing for bed, knowing the depression still ruled her and unable to make anything different happen.

"Catching the dirty agent is an important part of your survival." Connor reached across the table to clasp Sophie's hand. "You can't give up."

Sophie tugged her hand away. "Don't tell me what I can or can't do." She lifted up the surgical tape holding in the IV needle pressing into her skin and removed it. "I am aware I'm still depressed. I should have a session with Dr. Wilson, my therapist. Would you be willing to let us meet here?"

Connor frowned. "If it will make you feel better. Though I don't know what you'll say to explain how you're on Sheldon Hamilton's corporate jet at the Hilo Airport."

Sophie looked up and met his eyes. "You're the head of Security Solutions. You came and got me from my hiding place. It will be fine. But I don't have to lie. Dr. Wilson knows everything."

Connor blinked.

"Yes, everything. I needed a place to talk about all of my secrets. As a psychologist, she is bound by client confidentiality."

"I will just have to trust that that is enough."

"And if anything happens to her, I'll know who to go after."

Connor narrowed his eyes. "That you would think that of me shows how little you understand me and what I do, who I am."

"I don't know you at all, Connor, nor do I want to. You had your chance with me."

He winced, and she turned away, getting up from the dinette. "Thank you for breakfast, and for the medical care. I've got Dr. Wilson's number written down since my new phone isn't operational yet. Where are my personal items?"

"Your backpack is in the closet." He was clearing away the dishes. She saw pain in his rigid movements.

She couldn't soften toward him. She couldn't forgive him. *He'd let her grieve him, even go to a fake funeral!*

Sophie had written important numbers she wanted to keep on a tidy slip of paper rolled into her hiking boot. The boot was with the rest of her belongings, neatly stowed in a small, sealed cabinet in the bedroom. She had a much bigger list of contacts stored in the Cloud, but right now she was staying away from anything that could be tracked. She extracted the burner phone she hadn't been able to open before, grateful to find the battery included already held a charge. She programmed the phone, added Dr. Wilson's number to her contacts directory, and called her.

The psychologist's voicemail came on, and she left a message requesting an emergency session in an unusual location. "I'm sorry for the secrecy, Dr. Wilson, but that case I was on has exploded. I was in Witness Protection, which is why I hadn't been in touch for a while. Please come. Connor will send someone to get you and bring you to my location. And...I almost died from the depression. I decided to live, but it's so bad right now I'm not able to concentrate, to really care what happens, and I need to." Sophie rubbed the scar on her cheek. "I still need to make it to the Chang trial alive, and I'm having trouble caring about any of it."

She turned off the phone, dimmed the lights, and slid between the silky sheets, sinking into oblivion.

SOPHIE WAS on the helicopter Alika called the Dragonfly, swooping down toward a beautiful estate perched on the edge of a cliff overlooking Hanalei Bay on Kaua`i. She delighted in the stunning scene: the curve of the peaceful jade-green river, the punctuation of the historic red steel bridge, the patchwork quilt of taro fields, the great horseshoe arc of beach, and the sparkle of peaceful ocean.

"This is my home, and I want it to be your home too," Alika said.

Sophie gazed into his warm brown eyes, then down at the vista of ocean, valley, and sculptured green mountains as the helicopter landed gently and silently on the grass in front of a gracious plantation-style mansion. Her heart swelled with hope—and sorrow.

They weren't wearing helmets. The helicopter was silent, a bubble on the breeze.

"This is a dream. This isn't really happening."

"But it could," Alika said. Sophie looked over at him. Warmth flushed over her cold body.

Someone was shaking her shoulder.

"No, no." Sophie curled tight, shutting her eyes, clinging to the dissolving shreds of illusion.

"Wake up."

She finally unrolled and blinked resentfully up into Connor's dark brown eyes. "I hate your Sheldon Hamilton disguise."

"Too damn bad." Connor's face was a hard, unfamiliar mask. "The CIA is here to see you. Get up, get dressed, and get your shit together."

CHAPTER TWENTY-FIVE

SECRET SERVICE AGENT Ellie Smith and an unfamiliar man were seated on the dove-gray furniture of the lounge area of the jet. Sophie clutched the mug of hot, strong Thai tea Connor had plied her with the minute she was out of bed. He'd gone into his office and shut the door. Sophie felt a moment of panic facing the two without backup, until Ellie got up to greet Sophie, coming forward to give her a gentle hug. "You had us worried, young lady. Your father has been driving me crazy."

"I am sorry for the inconvenience." Sophie's lips felt stiff, her entire body rigid. The depression was barely in check. "I've been sick."

"You do look a little like a bear that just woke up before spring." The other man got up and came forward, reaching out to shake her hand. "Devin McDonald, at your service."

Sophie ignored his large, square hand. "Your ID, please, sir."

As she checked his identification wallet, she assessed him: mid-fifties, dressed in Hawaii business casual in chinos, an open-necked aloha shirt, and tan athletic shoes. McDonald had the ruddy complexion of a Caucasian with high blood pressure. After she checked his ID, she extended her hand and found that he had the handshake of someone who needed to assert dominance.

"In case you haven't guessed, we're here regarding the matter of your mother," Ellie said.

"First, I need to know how you knew where I was. I'm out of WITSEC, but I thought this was a secure location."

"Mr. Hamilton of Security Solutions reached out to your father to let him know you were safe; I was able to persuade him we could keep your whereabouts confidential."

Connor, taking the initiative again, managing her life. She wished she could feel more grateful.

Ellie sat down on the tufted leather sofa and Sophie did as well. "We were waiting for word from the agency about how to proceed, when you went dark."

Agent McDonald perched across from them on one of the leather flight loungers. "And finally, the agency decided to let me know about your dilemma," McDonald said. "I'm the closest thing to a supervisor the CIA has in Hawaii." He smiled, showing a lot of expensive veneers. "I understand your mother is an agent with the Yām Khûmkạn?"

"So she says." Sophie sipped the strong black tea, willing it to work, willing her foggy mind to focus. "She has made a crude attempt to recruit me for that organization."

"About that. What took the agency so long was the thorough research and background check they were working up on you. We are aware of your extensive background in technology, and the DAVID program. We have a thorough understanding of your career in law enforcement so far, and the reasons why a cabal like the Yām Khûmkạn might be interested in having someone like you in their organization."

"You are just restating things that I already know." Sophie tightened her grip on the warm mug. "Tell me something new."

"We are still investigating how bad the security breaches might have been with your father. He is taking a personal leave while this deep investigation takes place," Ellie said.

Sophie looked up to meet the agents' gazes. "So far you have answered what is going on with my father, and I appreciate that. One of the things I've been most concerned about is how this would affect him. But you still have not answered what I should do, or anything specific pertaining to my situation."

"No one can tell you what you should do, Sophie." Ellie's dark blue gaze was kind, an antidote to McDonald's flinty stare. "You are a free person. This is America. This is why we are a great nation. Even when our interests are threatened, we do our best to respect human rights. And Sophie is under no duress to take any one course of action, is she, Agent McDonald?"

"Not at this time." McDonald rubbed his hands together with a gentle whisking sound. "But that said, we would be most appreciative if you would penetrate the Yām Khûmkạn. We have had very little intel on the organization, its staff, or its mission. It would be a service to your country for you to get involved."

Sophie noted how carefully he avoided putting her role into words. "But I am under no obligation to do so?" Sophie probed, concerned that something about Connor and his secrets might be known to either of the agents.

McDonald blinked once, a slow settling of the eyelids like a reptile lazing in the sun. "Simple patriotism is not enough? I would think you'd want to prove your loyalty to the country that took you in after Assan Ang."

McDonald's reference to her abusive gangster husband rankled. "I am a United States citizen, lest you forget, and I have paid tenfold for that privilege by my service to the nation during my time with the FBI." Sophie shook her head. "I'm just making sure I'm not endangering my life by accepting—or refusing—your proposal."

"There are certainly concerns I have about you, your father, and the association both of you have with the Yām Khûmkạn through your mother. But until we know more, this is just a dialogue. A temperature check, if you will." McDonald bared his teeth in a perfunctory smile.

Sophie had to take his words at face value, though she sensed something threatening in McDonald's demeanor. There was no doubt in her mind that this interview would have had an entirely different tone if Ellie Smith hadn't been there to facilitate it. "I appreciate your coming to speak with me, and I will consider your request most carefully. But I'm afraid any further action regarding this situation is out of the question until the Chang trial is over. I have to stay hidden until then. There's a contract out on my life."

"We are aware of that, and if you agree to come to work for the Agency, we can take you in and squirrel you away until the trial is over. You will be completely safe, sequestered, paid and comfortable." McDonald's smile hadn't improved in appeal upon a third viewing. "What they call a twofer."

"Why don't you take some time to think about all of this, Sophie." Ellie stood up, evidently reading Sophie's expression. "You're still sick, and that's never the best time to think about major life decisions. Just know that your father and I are only a phone call away."

"Thank you, Agent Smith." Sophie drew a breath, let it out. "How is Ginger?"

"She's fine. Rambunctious as ever. She does seem to mope a bit, missing you, but don't worry. She is getting lots of love, and Jake comes by regularly to take her for walks with Tank."

Jake. And Tank. She missed her partner.

Sophie smiled. The expression felt unfamiliar, a clenching of muscles she had forgotten how to use. "I am glad to hear they are spending time with Ginger. It eases my mind to know she is cared for."

Sophie saw the two agents off the plane and went back to bed. She had just dimmed the lights when Connor appeared in the doorway. "You weren't going to tell me what went down out there?"

"You watched and listened to the whole thing on surveillance,"

Sophie said. "So there's nothing to tell." She tugged the silky comforter up around her shoulders and turned away, snuggling down to block out any light.

A beat went by.

"I'd like to know, in your own words, why we've just been visited by the Secret Service and the CIA." Connor's voice had gone frosty. In fact, ever since her comment to him at breakfast, his demeanor had shifted in a negative direction.

Sophie wanted to care but couldn't. She closed her eyes, fighting the desire to burrow even deeper into the covers. *How was she going to navigate this minefield, feeling as she did?*

Connor's voice softened. "Dr. Wilson is on her way. I sent a car for her."

"I hope she can help me."

"Sophie." Connor sat down on the edge of her bed. He reached out, picked up one of her cold hands, and chafed it. His were hard and cool, with calluses across the fingertips and in the web of his thumb from playing his violin. "I've never seen you like this. Even when you were shot, and recovering from that, you weren't like this."

"Even when I grieved your death I wasn't like this." And just like that, Sophie fell asleep, dropping instantly into a well of darkness.

CHAPTER TWENTY-SIX

Dr. Wilson sat in the largest lounger in the living room area, leaving the loveseat for Sophie. "It's not every day I get picked up by a limo and brought out to a private jet to do therapy. You said it was urgent. What's going on besides hiding from gangsters?"

"I hardly know where to begin." Sophie's tongue felt heavy. Her whole body ached. She hunched forward, her face in her hands. A long silence stretched out.

"I appreciate being able to meet the fascinating Connor, aka Sheldon Hamilton. He's quite good-looking, and such nice manners."

"I told him he couldn't watch this session." Sophie pointed to a tiny recessed button in the ceiling. "He did not reply." She took a small free-standing speaker out of her bag and synced it with her phone, playing a background of white noise. "In case he can't resist." She rubbed the scar on her cheekbone, unable to meet the psychologist's eyes. "I should never have canceled our appointments."

"That's not all of it. Tell me what happened out there on the lava when you were alone. Connor told me you almost died." Dr. Wilson's eyes were very blue. *Kind. Intelligent. Nonjudgmental.*

"Let me tell you what happened first that sent me out there."

Sophie described the attack that had almost killed Alika, and their resulting intimacy.

"What about Jake?" Dr. Wilson's slender blonde brows drew together as she echoed Marcella's question.

"What about Jake?" Defensiveness shaded her voice. "Jake knows we are not a couple. He told me that we wouldn't sleep together again unless I was willing to say we were exclusive. I refused. I owe him nothing." That wasn't strictly true, and she knew it.

Dr. Wilson's lips tightened. "I think he will be upset, nonetheless."

"I have bigger problems." Sophie would have rolled her eyes if she could have found the energy for it—*everyone seemed so concerned with Jake's feelings!* "I told Alika that I had been physically involved with Jake. Alika was the one who almost walked away from me. He was the one who had to make a choice to be with me. In spite of my…history."

"As long as you are honest with all involved, and everyone is making informed decisions." Dr. Wilson sat back, made a note on her pad. "At some point, that needs to include Jake."

"Being honest was your advice and I have followed it. It has not been easy." Sophie's gaze drifted to Connor's closed office door. Was he listening, watching? Probably. *He was not going to like what he was hearing.* "I left Alika early in the morning, cut off all communication, and went out to the WITSEC safe house. The depression got worse and worse out there. It became hard to function. Rayme was taken out by a shooter. I was shot at, too, and got a bunch of sizable splinters in my arm from a wooden railing. And so, I decided I was better off on my own with the leak in WITSEC still active. I assumed my Sandy Mason identity, handed Ginger off to Dad, and cut all ties. My plan was to hide out on a *kipuka* until the trial and recharge, maybe hike around some more out there off the grid, and undetectable. But what happened was…" Her voice trailed off.

"Another attack?" Dr. Wilson prompted.

"The depression attacked. First, I ran out of food…then water. I couldn't find the motivation to get up and leave, or the strength to open my new burner phone, or anything. I lost the will to live." Sophie looked down at her hands, ashamed. "Then I decided to… hasten the painful process of death by dehydration. I almost shot myself." The words fell into a pool of silence. Ripples seemed to spread outward from them. Sophie shut her eyes.

"What stopped you?" Dr. Wilson asked softly.

"Thinking of the grief my suicide would cause." Sophie looked up and met the psychologist's eyes. "I managed to contact Connor for help. He has the resources to have found me. He rescued me with a medical team and brought me here yesterday. I'm recovering physically, but I can't seem to shake off the depression. I need to stay alert and engaged through the trial, but I can't bring myself to care about…anything."

"Have you been taking your medication?"

"No." Sophie shook her head. "I misplaced it." Somewhere between the safe house and the *kipuka*, the bottle of little white pills had disappeared.

Dr. Wilson sighed. "You have a family history of depression, and a series of intense triggers have taken place. Your brain chemistry is severely impacted right now. I guessed that might be the case, so I brought along a medication people are calling "suicide first aid." Dr. Wilson produced a small green bottle with an aerosol pump top. "It's an anesthetic called ketamine that seems to perform a sort of chemical block to the worst of the depression. The effect is temporary, but temporary relief can give other interventions a chance to work."

Sophie twisted her fingers together. The attempt to warm her hands only reminded her of the bones in her fingers. She kept mentally seeing her phalanges, as if all that was left of her was her skeleton. "I didn't dare hope you had something that could help me," Sophie said. "because talking about this is making me worse. I've hurt so many people and let them down." She didn't realize she was crying until she felt tears drip off her chin, landing on her skeleton hands.

"That's the depression talking. Remember, the depression has a voice, a litany of accusations. Learn to recognize that voice and tune it out. But to facilitate that, this intervention is something you need right now."

"What do we do?" Sophie asked simply.

"The infusion is in a nasal spray. You'll do a couple of inhalations and then just lie back and rest. I'll do a little relaxation and visualization hypnosis narrative. You'll feel pleasantly relaxed, maybe a little sleepy. It takes about forty-five minutes for it to work."

"Forty-five minutes for me to be cured? Why haven't we done this sooner?" Sophie honestly wanted to know.

Dr. Wilson snorted a laugh. "You weren't my patient, before. And this treatment isn't FDA approved, so insurance won't cover it. But I'm fairly sure you'll feel some immediate relief from your symptoms. I'll have you use the spray daily. We can schedule follow up treatment if it works, until your life can get stabilized and you're able to make progress using more traditional methods."

Accepting the medication bottle with its atomizer top, Sophie followed Dr. Wilson's instructions, and inhaled several sprays of the medication, then reclined on the loveseat.

She immediately felt a tingly, pleasant sensation. She closed her eyes as Dr. Wilson began to speak. "Perhaps you'd like…to take a little time to just rest. Just letting go of all of your burdens. Breathing in relaxation, breathing out and releasing the tension, the stress, the fear, the despair. Breathing in peace, breathing out sadness. With every breath you take, you are completely and totally relaxing, enjoying, and surrendering to the process of healing that is beginning now."

As the psychologist's voice rose and fell in a gentle cadence, Sophie felt herself sinking deep into a quiet place within herself— but it wasn't that gray zone where nothing mattered. This place was warm and lit with golden light. *She was surrounded by love, supported and nurtured.*

Reality faded into warmth. She floated away on the sound of Dr. Wilson's voice.

⁂

"HOW ARE YOU FEELING?"

"Different." Sophie turned away from the small round window of the jet to face Dr. Wilson. After she'd had a restful nap, the psychologist had gently awakened her.

She did feel different.

That film that seemed to have separated her from the rest of the world had pulled back. She felt and heard the energy in her voice as she said, "Yes, I feel different."

Not happy. Not even content. But also, no longer half alive. She was fully operational, and her ability to focus had returned.

"I think the treatment worked. I feel like I can function."

"Good. The combination of hypnosis and ketamine infusion seems to be having a positive effect. I don't usually do this, but since access to you is a security risk, I'm going to give you the medication and have you self-administer. Try two sprays a day for a week; do a third if the effect wanes. You can take it before bed, since it makes you sleepy. Once you are stabilized and your situation resolved, we'll begin real therapy again." Dr. Wilson gave Sophie a hug. The psychologist stood back and held her at arm's length. "What one thing would make you feel better right now?"

"To see Alika again." Sophie did not know where the words had come from—they seemed to have sprung up out of somewhere deep and escaped her censoring mouth. She covered it with her hand and shut her eyes, terrified. *What had she just admitted?*

"Well, that could be problematic given your current situation," Dr. Wilson said, humor brightening her words. "What next thing would help?"

"To see Ginger." Sophie's eyes went misty at the thought of her dog.

"That's more doable." Dr. Wilson brushed imaginary lint off of Sophie's shoulders, a petting, comforting gesture. "I spoke to Connor. He is taking you to Oahu to await the trial. But he has agreed to fly you back here for your treatment and therapy as needed."

"That is most kind of him."

Dr. Wilson laughed. "I doubt very much that kindness is all there is to it. But you should take him up on his offer to look out for you. Oahu would be a much better setting for you to recover in than a tent in the wilderness with no food or water."

"It seems incredible that I went out there to evade Chang and almost ended up doing his work for him."

"Depression is a cunning and baffling disease. But promise me this: you will not isolate. It's bad for you right now."

"I promise." Sophie leaned into the psychologist's supportive embrace, then walked her to the door of the plane. Dr. Wilson waved as she went down the steps and got into the limo. "See you soon!" she called, and Sophie waved back.

CHAPTER TWENTY-SEVEN

"Dr. Wilson is a remarkable woman." Connor spoke at Sophie's shoulder as she watched the limo carrying the psychologist pull away across the tarmac.

"That she is. She gave me a treatment. It seems to be working. I feel much better. Clearer." Sophie turned to face him.

Connor was cool and dapper in his Hamilton persona, his eyes opaque, hidden by those glasses. "I'm glad. That's what we need. Why don't you have a bite to eat, and then we'll take off for Oahu."

"All right." Sophie followed Connor over to a small fridge.

He opened it, revealing two large plates of mixed vegetables, meat, and rice. "I took the liberty of ordering Thai food."

"Thank you." Sophie accepted a wrapped plate. "I am grateful for all you are doing to help me."

"Anything to support one of Security Solutions' best operatives." His emotional shutdown toward her was complete.

And that was good. She had told him not to hope she would change her mind about a relationship with him, and maybe he had gotten the message at last.

They ate at the dinette without speaking. Somehow, it felt comfortable in spite of all that lay between them. She had always liked that about being with Connor—hours could go by as they occupied the same space with no need for words.

She and Alika had shared that kind of restful presence with each other. Such a contrast to Jake, who wanted to know everything. Jake, who believed secrets were lies and always wanted to talk more than Sophie did.

Well, not always. Sometimes he just held her—warming and healing her without words, with just his body.

Jake. She felt guilty just thinking his name.

She had done the right thing by ending her physical involvement with him. He couldn't handle the secrets she had to carry and live with—secrets she'd never be able to share with him. *He should be with someone with a less complicated life.* She could imagine him with a nice white American woman and a house in the suburbs, Tank frolicking on the lawn.

Alika seemed able to allow Sophie to have a secret life, and not be threatened by it.

But she could not endanger him…

The black wingtips of hopelessness flickered at the edge of her vision, dragging at her thoughts. *She would not give in.* She was getting better! She had to be.

They stowed the disposable dishes and strapped into their seats. Sophie picked up a tablet and scrolled through the news as Connor greeted the pilots and discussed their plans up near the cockpit. He came back and settled himself beside Sophie in a lounger. He flipped a button on the console of his chair, speaking into an intercom. "We are ready for takeoff back here."

Sophie stared out the window at the palms swaying in a slight breeze, the ocean shrouded in the distance by the soft veil of Kilauea's volcanic emissions.

She wasn't going to get far keeping secrets from Connor. Secrets were his currency, his language, and she needed to know what he knew about the Yām Khûmkạn before going any further with the

CIA and her mother. He had never answered the question she had sent him on the Ghost software's chat function.

Sophie decided to take the plunge. "What do you know about the Yām Khûmkan?"

Connor's eyes widened slightly, the only indication he gave of any surprise. "Why do you ask?"

Sophie smiled, a humorless tightening of her lips. "I asked you first."

The jet's engines engaged, and the nimble craft moved out onto the runway. Connor did not answer as they were pressed back into their seats by the roar of acceleration.

Sophie waited until they were airborne to ask the question again. "What do you know about the Yām Khûmkan?"

"You opened this can of worms. I have something I want you to see." Connor rose from his seat and strode to the front of the plane in spite of their angle of ascension. He tapped on the pilot's door and disappeared. A few minutes later he returned to his seat. "Do you need anything? Hungry, thirsty?"

"No. I just want you to answer my question."

Connor sighed. "I am aware of the Yām. Sometimes our paths cross."

"Are they an organization that the Ghost has had dealings with?"

He sat down and glanced at Sophie. She still hated that his sea-blue eyes were hidden behind those brown contacts. "Sometimes they have been problematic. Sometimes they have been of service."

"Of service to whom?"

"Of service to the Ghost. Sometimes our interests align. Other times, they do not. Right now, they do not."

A terrible suspicion tightened Sophie's chest. Was Connor the source of the threat against the Thai royal family, and the reason her mother had been forced to seek her out? "Tell me more."

"Why should I?" His face was expressionless. "You have amply demonstrated your attitude about me. And my activities."

"I have also demonstrated a healthy respect for those activities, and an acknowledgment of their utility by asking for your help on cases that cannot be solved in the usual way, including the WITSEC leak."

Connor did not reply. He looked out the window.

The plane leveled off. Sophie unbuckled and got up, heading to the little kitchenette. She opened one of the cupboards. Her favorite, hard-to-find brand of tea had been stocked, and though she was not surprised, it gave her a little sting anyway. She filled an electric teakettle and turned back to face Connor.

He was working on a touchscreen tablet, his head bent, his fingers flying.

"Would you like some tea?" Sophie felt another pang, realizing that it was the first time she had offered him anything, tried to do anything for him. She owed him so much.

"No, thank you." Connor did not look up.

Was he on the Ghost software? Curiosity felt like an unused muscle after the deadening of her depression. She looked around the immaculate space with its buttery leather furnishings as if seeing it for the first time. "Where is Anubis?"

"My dog does not care for flying."

Ginger loved being anywhere Sophie was, and that would include flying. *She should never have given up her dog.* She would never have gotten to such a dark place out on that *kipuka* with her beloved Lab to care for...

The kettle beeped. She poured the water and added tea in an insulated metal mug. She rejoined Connor at his seat. He turned down his tablet and gazed at her. "Why are you asking about the Yām Khûmkạn?"

"I have heard from my Thai relatives recently. It came up in conversation." Sophie sipped the scalding tea carefully.

"That seems unlikely."

He was reading her evasion. *Could she trust him with the truth?*

But wasn't she already trusting him with her life? And if she would be going against him by further entanglement with her mother, it was a battle she was likely to lose. Perhaps she could turn the whole situation into something she could control.

Sophie set the mug into the leather chair's cup holder. "All right. I was approached by my mother. She is not depressed after all, nor in an institution. She is an agent of the Yām Khûmkạn."

Connor raised his brows. "Is that so?"

"Yes. She approached me some weeks ago. She told me that my skills are needed to combat enemies attacking the Yām Khûmkạn and their interests. It occurred to me that there may be a conflict between the Yām Khûmkạn and the Ghost."

"You are correct." Connor laid his hand over hers where it rested on the arm of the seat. "Thank you for trusting me with the truth. I hoped you would, eventually."

Bile rushed up, closing Sophie's throat, forcing her to swallow. *Did he already know everything that was going on?* "Are you going to make me regret trusting you?"

"Haven't I done all that I can to help you, to support you, to save your life, even? Didn't I tell you I love you?" Connor took off his glasses as if to see her better, but the brown contacts were still a layer of deception between them.

Sophie pulled her hand out from under his. She looked away and took a calming sip of her tea. "That is why I decided to tell you. I do not know how to handle Mother's request. The CIA agent was here because I am considering becoming an asset, an informant for them. But I cannot do anything for anyone until after the Chang trial, and that gives me a little time to consider my options. I have to call my mother soon, though, and explain why I haven't responded, give her something to keep her waiting until I am ready to make a decision."

"You need to stay far away from Pim Wat. She is not who you think she is."

"I already know that." Sophie stared out the window at the deep blue sky racing by, the clouds far below.

"Pim Wat is not only a spy, she is an assassin. One of the deadliest in the world. She specializes in poisons that mimic natural causes."

Sophie turned to look at Connor, her heart pounding. Her eyes felt dry, her hands clammy. "How do you know this?"

"After I left the states, I went to Thailand. I was curious about your family, and the issues of Thailand, so I put the Ghost to work checking into things. There is a wealth of corruption in that country, and at its heart is the Yām Khûmkạn—and your mother is one of their weapons. Wherever she went with your father, death followed —undetected. The Yām Khûmkạn found a way to use her that worked with her limitations."

Sophie gulped her tea, and it burned her tongue. The insulated metal mug rattled against her teeth. She wrapped both hands around the cup, seeking warmth. *If her mother was such a great assassin, why hadn't she killed Assan Ang and freed her daughter?* "Even the CIA did not know what you are telling me."

"That's true. Though they do know more than McDonald told you."

"So, you listened in on my meeting with Agent McDonald." It shouldn't feel like a betrayal, yet it did. "Did you listen to my therapy with Dr. Wilson, too?"

"What did you expect?" Connor's voice was sharp as he got up. "This is my world you're in. I see and know everything that goes on in my world." He headed into the kitchenette. "I think I will have some tea after all."

"You told me you wouldn't listen to my therapy. I put on white noise." She knew she sounded childish. She stared at the well-cut black shirt showcasing Connor's v-shaped back and remembered how good he looked naked. She was unmoved by the imagery.

"There are speakers embedded in the seats. Nothing goes on around me that I don't know about." His back was still toward her. *Yes, it was always best to assume he knew everything.*

She glanced out the window. The clouds appeared as downy feathers floating above the muted blue of the ocean. "Shouldn't we be descending already?" The plane flight from Hilo to Honolulu was a thirty-minute hop.

"I told you I wanted to show you something. We will be flying for a while." Connor's back was still toward her as he fussed with the tea makings. "Taking you somewhere other than Oahu solves a number of problems. I will bring you back to see Dr. Wilson if necessary, and we'll return for the trial."

Sophie's heart kicked into overdrive. "I did not agree to come to wherever it is that you are taking me."

"It is for your own good."

"I will be the judge of that." She indulged in a brief fantasy of fighting him, of kicking his ass MMA style—*but it would never work.* She was a shadow of her usual strength right now.

Connor walked toward her and sat down with his cup of tea, calm as ever. "You are not safe to be alone. And you are not safe to be anywhere that the Changs and their thugs can find you. You're the one who brought up your home country. I thought we should go to my place in Thailand. Perhaps you will find some of the answers you seek there."

Sophie rubbed the scar on her cheek. Frustration and inner conflict tied her tongue. "So, you were waiting for me to bring up my mother and the Yām Khûmkạn. You already researched her and that organization. You've already had dealings with them. When were you going to tell me?"

"When you asked me about it." Connor sipped his beverage. "I suspected your mother was going to make contact with you when I tracked her to the Big Island. But I chose not to interfere. She is your mother, after all."

"She's a stone-cold evil bitch," Sophie spat. "The Ghost could do something about that."

Connor sat perfectly still. "And you would forgive me for 'doing something about' your mother, without your consent or knowledge?"

Sophie groaned, leaning forward to cover her face with her hands. "Yes. No. I don't know."

"So you see why I waited for you to come to me about her and the situation with the Yām Khûmkạn. There was no other way for me to approach it."

"You could have contacted me. Told me. I would have wanted to know what you knew."

"And you'd have thought I was trying to turn you against your mother. You'd have hated me for anything I tried to tell you about her. It's called 'shoot the messenger,' Sophie, and I knew you'd want someone to blame. No, it had to play out the way it has." He took another maddeningly calm sip of tea.

"But you told me she's an assassin, not just a spy." Sophie glared at him, knowing he was right.

"That was so that you could be safe. I wouldn't put anything past Pim Wat. She wants you now, for her own purposes. But just like the CIA, I don't trust that those purposes have your best interests at heart."

"And you do? Have my best interests at heart?" Sophie couldn't help the words that burst out of her. "Because it sure didn't seem like it when I wept at your memorial service until you walked up to give your own eulogy."

"Everything I do has a purpose. And ultimately, you are a part of that purpose. I wish you would let that whole thing go and trust me."

"How could I?" Sophie looked out the window. "It's easiest to just assume that you're manipulating everything for one of your games. Including me. Including my mother, and the Yām Khûmkạn, and the CIA, and maybe even the Changs…"

"You give me a lot of credit." He grinned. "I like it. Wait and see about your mother, and the Changs, and even this contract on your life. Things have a way of working out."

Secrets hid behind Connor's brilliant white smile, and Sophie knew she'd learned all she was going to for the moment.

CHAPTER TWENTY-EIGHT

BYRON CHANG STARED into his brother Akane's dark brown eyes. Objectively, he knew they were the same as his: slightly almond-shaped, a brown so dark the pupil was hard to see, with rounded, thick black brows. Yet the expression in Akane's eyes was so different: flat, dead, as if there were a spark missing.

When had that spark disappeared? Had jail stolen it, or had it been gone for years? Truth was, Byron couldn't remember the last time he had spent time alone with his little brother.

Akane had bulked up in the shoulders from working out, and a new tattoo, likely some gangster symbol, peeked out of the collar of his orange jumpsuit. He turned his head the better to display it, and Byron recognized the crude shape of a shark wrapped around his throat. His brown skin was reddened with irritation around the tattoo site, and Byron worried briefly about infection.

Worrying about his little brother was an ingrained habit he needed to lose.

"Like what you see?" Akane raised his brows. "It's my *aumakua.*"

"We don't have an *aumakua.*" The Changs were part Hawaiian, but the cultural belief in an ancestral guardian spirit had never been a part of their family history.

"Speak for yourself. Mine is a tiger shark."

"Tats have never been my thing." Byron narrowed his gaze. "I haven't visited you in here."

"I noticed."

"There was a reason."

"I figured. Big bruddah always has a reason for everything." Akane's voice dripped sarcasm. He wasn't chained or cuffed; the county jail was not a high security facility. They were separated by a metal table and had been given a private room; that was all the pull Byron had been able to exert for this meeting. "You can tell me your reason whenever you're ready. I've got all day."

"I needed to distance myself, and our business, from the media shitstorm around your arrest. Things have died down a bit, thank God. I'm doing all I can to get you out."

"Doesn't seem like it from my end. The lawyer you sent is a bitch."

"She's the best defense lawyer in Hawaii. You have to be patient with the process. And, given how far from the family's interests you've gone, you're lucky I don't just leave you in here to rot." Byron's fists clenched at the scrutiny Akane's penchant for murder had brought to the Chang operation. "I shouldn't have to clean up your shit, bro, and you shouldn't shit where you eat."

Akane tipped his head back and laughed, a full belly laugh of genuine amusement. The sound brought "chicken skin" up on Byron's arms. "What's so funny?"

"You. Telling me to do your dirty work, and then objecting to the way it gets done. You made me what I am, *bro*."

The hair on Byron's arms had not settled. His mind flashed to Terence Chang, in his office, asking who was going to manage a rabid dog without being bitten.

"Don't make me regret all I'm doing to get you out of here," Byron hissed, leaning forward. "I can still say the word and you'll be shipped off to federal prison in Nowhere, Nebraska for multiple life sentences. It would be no more than you deserve, you sick fuck."

Akane laughed again.

Byron shot to his feet. "Shut up!"

"Follow your conscience, bro, if you still have one. I've done away with mine. Found it cramped my style." Akane stood up, turned his back on Byron in blatant disrespect, and pounded on the door. "Guard! We're done here."

Akane had to know who was boss.

Byron launched himself across the room, grabbed Akane by the back of the neck, and banged his brother's head into the door just as the guard struggled to open it.

Akane threw back his elbow to hit Byron in the solar plexus. As Byron bent, gasping, Akane spun and hit him with an uppercut.

Byron reeled, then hurled himself at his brother, pummeling. All was a chaos of whirling, grappling, and crashing into the walls and the bolted-down table as the brothers fought.

Suddenly Byron lost all motor function—his body convulsed, his eyes rolled back, and he crashed to the ground, twitching, bolts of lightning flashing red behind his eyeballs.

WHEN HE CAME AROUND, Byron was lying on the floor. His ears rang. His head pounded. His bowels felt suspiciously loose. He hoped he hadn't shamed himself. He tried to sit up but his limbs refused to cooperate.

He blinked bleary-eyed at the corrections officer leaning over him. "Take it easy. You've been tased. You'll feel better soon," the guard said. "You're lucky I'm not keeping you overnight and slapping you with assault charges. You can thank my uncle Neville with a little bonus in his paycheck."

The CO, whom he recognized as related to one of his meth

factory workers, helped him up off the floor. "Thanks." Byron forced his lips to form words. "It's done."

"And I'll further spin it that you kicked the shit out of your nutbag brother," the guard said. "But that'll be extra. Because from what I saw, it was Akane kicking *your* ass."

Byron couldn't find words to respond. *It was true.* A few minutes more, and Akane would have knocked him out, likely killed him if he could.

This could not get out. It would damage his reputation as head of the family. Some would say he wasn't strong enough to lead; some might even want Akane in his place. *And that would be a terrible thing.* For everyone.

"Got you covered," Byron lisped through numb and tingly lips.

The CO stood aside. "Glad we could help each other."

Byron shook his head slowly and shambled for the door. Outside the jail, he fired up the black Tundra he drove and cranked up the AC. He was sweaty and trembling, his body still sending out jangled distress signals, his mind abuzz with terrified thoughts.

"Son of a bitch," he muttered. "Holy shit."

Akane was going to kill him the first chance he got. Kill him, and take his job running the family—and Akane didn't have the business sense of a coqui frog. The man had cunning, but no smarts. Byron couldn't let that happen.

Heart rate finally calming, Byron fetched his phone, stowed in the locked glove box. Text messages blinked at him. He worked his way through them, the process of resuming the reins of his authority calming him. He was important, needed. *He was the boss.*

A final text message. He thumbed it open. *"Call off the hit on the woman, or you won't have a family left to protect."* UNKNOWN showed in the phone's window.

Byron's heart thudded like a sledgehammer. No one had this phone contact info but his most trusted lieutenants—not even his wife had this number!

"Shit." He had already decided to pull the job on the woman.

Akane needed to cool off in jail—maybe forever. But if he pulled the plug, would he lose face with an unknown enemy? Would threats and blackmail attempts come his way because he appeared to comply, showed weakness? "Give an inch and they'll take a mile," his uncle, patriarch Terry Chang, used to say.

Byron stared at the phone in his hand as he groped for a solution. *He had to contact the Lizard.*

His skin crawled at the memory of the letter opener at his throat. He'd hoped never to speak to that piece of filth again. *And what if the Lizard refused to cooperate?*

But either way, this call had to be made. He would spin the fallout as best he could.

Byron pressed a preprogrammed number and put the phone to his ear, listening to it ring.

CHAPTER TWENTY-NINE

THAILAND'S AIR WAS BALMY, and even more humid than Hawaii's. Fragrances, strangely familiar in spite of the reek of jet fuel, tickled Sophie's nostrils as she stood at the open door of the jet. The sun overhead was bright after the dim, climate-controlled environment inside, and she squinted, shielding her eyes to look around.

Somehow the jet had been able to land on a short runway bordered by grass, palm trees, a dazzling white sand beach, and an aquamarine ocean.

Connor handed her a pair of sunglasses and a hat. "You'll have to watch out for sun stroke."

"You forget. I was born here." Sophie felt a sort of humming recognition in her bones. Though she'd never seen this particular place, her spirit recognized home. "Which island is this?"

"It's called Phi Ni. My private island." Connor shrugged, elaborately casual. His voice was gruff, but she heard something new in it, a note of pride and underlying excitement.

Why would she be surprised? Of course, Connor would have a private island here in Thailand. Her homeland contained many places far from the prying eyes and reaching tentacles of any government.

Sophie descended the steps and he followed her, carrying a

couple of duffel bags. He handed her one of them. "I picked up a few things for you before we left the States. Some clothing appropriate to your Mary Watson persona. I thought you could be her while you're here, pass yourself off as my personal assistant."

At least he wasn't setting her up to appear as his girlfriend. "That is acceptable." Sophie took the duffel bag and followed as Connor led her to a parked Jeep. "No limousine?" Her lips twitched in a smile.

Connor smiled back. "I save that for when I'm trying to impress a lady. You're a lost cause at this point." The hint of humor took the sting from the words, and they were nothing more than true.

Sophie smiled. "Does this mean we can be friends now?"

"No. I intend to pout a while longer." He stuck his lower lip out comically, and Sophie remembered the playful personality he'd cultivated as Todd Remarkian, and how much she'd enjoyed that. He really was a chameleon, and one in a billion. *Too bad he'd broken her love for him.*

Sophie craned her neck to take in the sights and smells as the Jeep bumped down a crushed coral road. Grasses gave way to jungle and coconut trees. The air was filled with barely remembered birdsong and the high-pitched calling of tree frogs and an occasional monkey shriek. "Does anyone else live on this island?" Sophie clutched Mary Watson's sun hat as they hit a bump.

"Not if I can help it."

"Don't tell me you got all this with honest money?"

He slanted a glance at her. "Let's just say the money was never missed and is doing more good here than it would have done there."

"Ah-ha. I got a glimpse of that skim you were running on those nefarious accounts when I was in the Ghost database."

"Those accounts will never miss a few billion. I was careful. Most of it went to charity. This place was my gratuity."

"Quite a gratuity," Sophie said, as they crested a ridge and his house came into view.

Built of bamboo and native woods in a combination of Balinese

WIRED SECRET

and plantation styles, the house was perched on the edge of a cliff overlooking a half-moon of crystalline bay. Sharply peaked roofs surrounded a central courtyard in the Thai style, while a wide, wrap-around porch with large windows overlooking the bay below embraced the Western aesthetic.

"It is beautiful, Connor." Sophie got out of the Jeep where Connor parked it beside a large barn filled with recreational vehicles of various kinds. "So this is where you've been when you were Sheldon Hamilton, international man of mystery."

"Yes," he said simply.

The front door, an imposing structure of deep red wood carved in intricate patterns of fish, animals, and flowers, was opened by a smiling older man in a simple smock and pants. Stone lions in the Asian style flanked the door, snarling in defense of the gracious home.

Anubis squeezed past the manservant and bounded down the carved stone steps, his whole body vibrating with happiness to see his master. Sophie couldn't help smiling as Connor knelt and embraced the usually dignified Doberman. "I missed you, too, boy."

Anubis wheeled to press his lithe body against Sophie's legs, his cropped hind end wagging, and her eyes stung as she stroked the Doberman's sleek head. She'd cared for the beautiful dog for some time, and they'd formed a bond. Still, petting him reminded Sophie of her dog. "I miss Ginger. She would love this place and being with Anubis."

"I could send the plane," Connor said. "Call your father and let him know. I'll send a guy to get her."

Sophie blinked moisture from her eyes. Her heart seemed to swell, an odd sensation. "You would do that?"

"Your happiness matters to me." Connor held her gaze with blue-green eyes she'd thought she was in love with. Now that he was on his own turf, he'd discarded the disguise she hated and only Sheldon Hamilton's brown hair remained. "Just say the word."

"Please get Ginger. She would be so happy to see Anubis. She is more social than I am. She really likes Tank, the dog Jake and I rescued on our last case." Sophie felt her tongue tripping over an unexpected gush of words as she followed Connor up the steps onto the landing. *She couldn't wait to see her dog.* "Ginger loves my dad, but Ellie said she still waits for me."

"Consider it done."

Sophie was surreptitiously dashing tears off her cheeks as Connor turned to introduce her to his manservant. "Nam, this is Mary Watson, my executive assistant. Mary, this is Nam. He helps everything run smoothly in my home here on Phi Ni."

Sophie bowed slightly to Nam, her hands folded. *"It is a pleasure to meet you, sir,"* she said in Thai.

The man's eyes widened in surprise, and he bowed in return. *"It is always a pleasure to speak my native tongue with a servant of my master."*

Sophie suppressed a cringe at being called Connor's servant. *"Indeed. Thank you for your hospitality."*

Nam took their bags and shuffled off. Sophie followed Connor into a long, narrow great room overlooking the central courtyard area of the house. Floor-to-ceiling sliding glass windows fronted a cascading fountain that filled the house with the gentle sound of running water. A statue of Quan Yin poured water from an urn into a pool at her feet.

"A beautiful work of art." Sophie pointed to the fountain. Done in some gleaming white stone, it seemed to glow in its setting of tropical plants and ferns.

"I am partial to goddesses." Connor slanted her a glance. "Human and otherwise."

"Ha. I am no gentle Quan Yin." *This was getting too personal.* Sophie walked forward and slid the door open to walk through the courtyard. Connor followed.

He touched her arm and pointed to sliders screened by window coverings on either side of the garden area. "These are bedrooms, and my office and home gym are on the other side. Straight ahead are the kitchen, dining room, and living room areas." He stepped in front of her and opened the door on the opposite side of the courtyard. "After you."

The living room overlooked a veranda that she had glimpsed from outside, with a cantilevered deck protruding over the limestone bluff upon which the house was built. One side contained a dining room table with four chairs which faced the view, and the other contained a sleek lounger facing a flat screen TV. Sophie appreciated the space aesthetically. Connor had good taste—one of the things she liked about him.

Sophie gestured. "So, you do watch television on occasion."

"I am always sifting information, usually online. But I do like to watch the occasional movie." Connor picked up a remote and hit a button. A set of metal blackout blinds rattled down over the huge windows. "In case of storms, bullets, or too much sun for my home theater."

Anubis pressed against Sophie's leg, and she petted the dog absently as she smiled. "I get the feeling you haven't had occasion to show this place off much."

"You are my first guest." Connor said it so matter-of-factly that the lack of emphasis was, in itself, a statement.

Sophie walked over to the glass sliders as he retracted the metal blind once more. She slid one door open and stepped out onto the deck, gasping at the beauty.

Spectacular stone atolls topped with vegetation punctuated the crystal-clear bay below. The water was so clear that the white sand bottom made it glow like chalcedony. She leaned on the railing and felt a sense of flying. The blue horizon seemed to stretch so far away she could see the bend of the earth.

"A penny for your thoughts." Connor joined her at the railing. His shoulder brushed hers. That used to thrill her, and the memory of what they'd lost brought a wave of sadness.

Sophie moved away. "I rather think they are worth more than a penny."

He smiled. "A million dollars then."

She frowned at him. "That is inappropriate." She looked back out over the bay, into the infinity of a smudged blue horizon. "My thoughts are that this is almost too beautiful, and it feels very good to be home in my country. You must have known that it would."

"I hoped so. And if I want to give you a million dollars to hear your thoughts, there's not a thing you can do to stop me."

Sophie turned to face him fully. "That is not the right tone to take with me, Connor. I do not tolerate dominance. It has left a bitter taste in my mouth."

Connor turned away, resting his elbows on the railing beside her, saying nothing for a long time.

Finally, he spoke. "I could say I was joking, and I was, but it was the wrong tone to take, as you say. I have been alone here too long. Let's go for a swim, and you can say hello to the ocean creatures of your homeland."

CHAPTER THIRTY

DAYS DRIFTED by like sand sifting through an hourglass: effortlessly, easily, and too quickly. Ginger arrived, ecstatic to see her mistress, soothing Sophie's ragged nerves with her joyful enthusiasm. The dog would not be parted from Sophie's side for even a moment after her arrival.

Sophie ate beautiful, delicious food and walked for hours on the empty beaches of the island with Ginger and Anubis, picking up shells, as Connor worked in his computer cave. She slept in the sun and swam in the warm bath of the ocean. She and Connor ran at night with the dogs when the heat of the day had receded, often enjoying the gentle waves and a swim in the sea.

Sitting on her pareu on the beach and meditating one morning, Sophie listened to the cry of the birds and the shush of the water. Ginger lay beside her on one side, Anubis on the other. She felt the breeze, scented with jasmine, caress her bare skin—the bikini Connor had provided was barely decent, a couple of scraps of fabric held together by strings. But there was no one to see or judge, and she felt almost naked in it, a comfortable state.

She was safe here, and like a sponge that had been severely

wrung out, she was refilling again with the calm, comfort, safety, and plenty that surrounded her.

Sophie heard the swish of Connor walking through the sand, felt his presence beside her, heard his murmur to Anubis as he sank to sit beside his dog on the sand. She felt his gaze on her body, and the hum of his hunger for her.

She heaved a mental sigh.

Connor had been respectful of her personal space. The companionship they'd enjoyed previously as they worked and played side by side seemed to have been restored. She was ready to forgive him, just for bringing Ginger here.

But she was no longer attracted to him.

"I found a vapor trail." Connor broke the soothing silence.

A 'vapor trail' was Connor's vernacular for a digital signature. Sophie opened her eyes and glanced at him. He was staring out over the turquoise water, just beginning to be ruffled by the morning breeze.

"Attached to the WITSEC Trojan?"

"Yes. I think I found the lead we've needed to track the data siphon. I've developed a tag that will send me information about who is accessing the Trojan. I was hoping you would check the coding before I uploaded it."

Sophie met his blue-green gaze. "You don't need me to check your coding."

"But I want you to."

Sophie had lost interest in the case, in anything but feeling good in the moment. She had used Dr. Wilson's nasal spray only a couple of times since her arrival. They had discussed the case often over meals, and she knew she needed to reengage with the world and its dirt and danger. She struggled to find motivation, to put her ennui into words. "I'm too lazy."

"Then I need to show you something. What I really brought you here for."

Sophie shut her eyes, wishing she could stay in the fragile, ephemeral bubble of peace and beauty he'd wrapped her in. *It was an illusion, bought at a high price by the Ghost.* "All right." She stood, shook out her pareu, and wrapped it around her body. "Let's go."

Sophie was warm and flushed by the time she reached the top of the precipitous stairs leading to the house from the beach. Connor was scarcely out of breath, but both dogs flopped in the shade of the house, panting, as they entered the cool of the stone-flagged courtyard.

"We're taking my chopper. I need you to get into a flight suit," Connor said.

CHAPTER THIRTY-ONE

Sophie had met Connor's pilot—he only had a few staff at the house, and they often ate with them for meals. A mixed Thai and American of short stature and composed mien, Thom Tang handed Sophie her helmet as she climbed into the lightweight, bubble-fronted helicopter. "You sit up front with Thom," Connor said. "This trip is for you."

He climbed into the rear jump seat of the chopper first and strapped in behind Sophie and the pilot as they got settled.

"Where are we going?" Sophie frowned, adjusting her harness.

Thom activated the rotors, and soon the noise was too loud for conversation except through the built-in mic of the helmet. "You'll see," Connor said through the tinny feed.

Condescending son of a yak! She really hated surprises.

The flare of anger that she felt was the first strong emotion she'd experienced since they'd arrived on the island, and the unfamiliar spark made her realize the depression was better. Its deadening hold had rolled back enough to allow a greater range of feeling.

Thom pulled back gently on the collective, and the helicopter rose off the gravel pad behind Connor's storage barn. Sophie leaned forward to see out of the curving Plexiglas, taking in a soaring view of towering bluffs and wild jungle plunging to the calm sea. The island was a rough triangle shape that drew down to a low-elevation point where the airstrip was. Sophie held her breath, her stomach dropping, as the chopper swung out over the cliff where Connor's house was perched.

Once again, she appreciated the dwelling's architecture and how he had designed it, staining the wooden sections in the tones of stone and earth so that it seemed to grow from the bluff in a way that harmonized with its surroundings.

They dropped down a bit, flying low over the rugged islets and knobs of stone peppering translucent blue water. "You have the coordinates?" Connor asked Thom.

"Roger that," Thom said.

Connor touched Sophie's arm, getting her attention. "We're going to the mainland so you can see the main temple of the Yām Khûmkạn."

"Temple?" Sophie's pulse picked up at the mention of her mother's clandestine organization. "The group has a central meeting place?"

"The Yām Khûmkạn is as much a cult as anything. Recruits live at the temple for close to a year and are subjected to rigorous training in a number of disciplines."

"How did you find all this out?" Sophie turned to make eye contact with Connor through the barrier of her helmet.

He merely raised his brows. "I have my ways."

"Indeed you do, *foul breath of a crocodile*." Sophie resented his doling out of information about something so personal. *There was so much he wasn't telling her!*

"What's that?"

"Nothing. Just getting ready to investigate this cultural wonder."

"There are binoculars beside your seat," Thom said helpfully. "We'll be there in half an hour."

Sophie took out the binoculars and scanned the mainland coastline of Thailand as it rapidly approached them, taking in a village with its fishing docks and simple dwellings, rice paddies, winding dirt roads. Cars were few and far between—most people traveling were on bikes or motor scooters, and there were even a few ox-drawn carts.

The dense green of jungle, bisected by one of the many rivers, soon obscured any signs of civilization, but Sophie continued to scan the ground with its swelling hills. This area was more rugged than the domesticated countryside near Bangkok, where she'd grown up on the Ping River.

A large square defined by a high wall appeared suddenly. No road that Sophie could see from above led to the magnificent edifice filled with tall, pointed, ornately decorated stone buildings in the Thai style.

They flew around the perimeter and Sophie scanned the temple with the binoculars, taking in an elaborately crenellated building. The building material was streaked with age and lichens, testifying to the age of the compound. A central courtyard before the massive main building bustled with figures dressed in black, performing martial arts exercises in neat rows. Miniature versions of the main temple were replicated as outbuildings, all enclosed within an impressive wall that held back encroaching jungle.

Sophie leaned as close as she could to the glass so she could take in all she could see—and recoiled as she spotted a cluster of black-clad inhabitants running out of one of the buildings with guns. One of the figures was aiming a rocket launcher in their direction, the large black tube on his shoulder pointed right at them. "Get us out of here, Thom!" Connor yelled.

The pilot veered the collective to the left just in time as the men below opened fire with machine guns. A hissing roar announced a missile whizzing by, narrowly missing them. Sophie clutched her harness as the helicopter heeled over, diving toward the cover of a nearby hill.

The missile detonated in the air near them with a sound like the world ending.

Sophie opened her mouth in a silent scream as the chopper was hurtled sideways, propelled by the blast. Connor cursed, Thom prayed in Thai, and Sophie shut her eyes, drawing deep inside herself to that calm dim place.

To think she'd fought so hard and long against so many enemies, only for it to end like this...

The helicopter rotated end to end, a dizzying sensation. The rotors screamed with the strain. "We're not hit," Thom yelled. "It's the backwash from the explosion. She just needs to get her bearings..."

Sophie opened her eyes. *Hell if she was going to let the depression take anything more from her, even one minute of suffering, if that was all that was left of life!*

The chopper continued to spiral down toward the jungle. Bile crawled up Sophie's throat as her stomach rebelled against the gyrations. Monkeys fled the path of their descent, swinging away across the tops of the trees as the whirling juggernaut plummeted toward them.

The spinning slowed, and just as suddenly as it had started, cavitation ceased. Thom straightened the collective and pointed it forward. The trees were so close that Sophie could see individual leaves by the time the chopper responded, lifting up and away.

"*Foul goiter on the devil's backside!* You should have anticipated that they'd be armed, Connor!" Sophie turned in her seat, only to see that Connor had removed his helmet and was retching into a gear bag.

She looked away and swallowed, calming her own stomach with an effort as Thom arrowed the helicopter at top speed out across the jungle toward the ocean. Eventually Connor's voice came back on the comm.

"You're right. The Yām Khûmkạn don't keep much information online; I wasn't able to hack the temple's defenses and obtain a map or schematic, because they don't use any known security programs. All I had been able to determine was the temple's use and location.

We should have kept a low profile instead of just buzzing them like that."

"And now they know someone's watching them," Sophie said. "Do you think we should fly right back to your island? What if they have radar or something, and can track where we're going?"

"I'll land us in Phi Phi." Thom named a larger island popular among visitors. "There are many tourists there. They should not be able to track us once we land in the busy airport. This chopper just looks like one of a thousand tour aircraft."

Connor was silent as they flew the extra distance and Thom radioed the airport with their flight plan. They landed in a bustling helicopter area, loud with engines and ripe with the smells of fuel and chatter of voices.

Sophie could hardly wait to get out of the helicopter. She took off her helmet as the rotors slowed and waited for Connor as he and Thom conferred.

Finally, the two got out and Thom began checking over the helicopter.

Connor walked toward Sophie, carrying his helmet and the befouled gear bag. He still looked pale and a little green, and Sophie smiled. "I think you have been punished for this mistake already."

"That was too close," Connor said. "Thom's going to have the mechanics check over our aircraft for damage and refuel it." He held up the bag. "And I'm disposing of this."

They walked to a metal-roofed private hangar that had been outfitted for passengers as a lounge. Sophie found a women's restroom and, after checking that it was empty, used the facilities and splashed water on her face.

Connor wasn't the only one looking a little worse for wear after their recent experience. She shed her flight suit; there was no air conditioning in the building, and palm frond ceiling fans did little but move the humid air around. The tank top and exercise shorts she wore underneath were fine for this setting.

The hangar was outfitted with a drinks area decorated with stools covered in bright colors. A grass skirt fronting the bar gave a tropical feel. Connor, also out of his flight gear, gestured Sophie over and handed her a tall, frothy, aqua-colored drink trimmed with a carved bamboo skewer laden with peeled rambutan. "A Blue Hawaiian. Or, as close as the bartender could get."

"Divine nectar of the gods!" Sophie sucked down a sweet, refreshing sip. "My favorite drink. The perfect antidote to our misadventure."

"I'm learning Thai, and I think I understood that. Something about the gods?" Connor clinked his beer against the rim of her drink. "I can't apologize enough."

"It was almost worth it to see the Ghost get airsick," Sophie said, a smile tugging her lips. "I never thought I'd see you 'lose your cool,' as Marcella would say."

Connor pushed his short dark hair back with a hand, shaking his head. "Well, now we know that the Yām Khûmkạn is ready, willing, and able to take down anyone or anything they see as a threat. We looked like an innocent tourist helicopter, and they showed no hesitation in trying to shoot us right out of the sky."

Sophie shivered, remembering the violent spinning of the helicopter, the sight of the monkeys fleeing an imminent crash into the jungle canopy. She lifted her Blue Hawaiian. "To good pilots."

"And guardian angels that work overtime." Connor clinked his glass to hers, and they drank.

CHAPTER THIRTY-TWO

CONNOR'S COMPUTER lab had no windows except a set of sliding glass doors that faced into the courtyard, covered by a set of light-filtering blinds. Entering the space for the first time the next day, Sophie smiled at the sight of his workstation; she was familiar with even the gym equipment and violin practice areas in the room, because the layout was a replica of his secret "Bat Cave" office in the Pendragon Arches building in Honolulu.

"You don't need me for any of this," Sophie said as she walked over and sat in a luxurious ivory leather office chair in front of three monitors and two computers that he had set up for her. "You're just making an excuse to get me working again."

"True. But everything is more fun when it's shared. I did not know that before I met you," Connor said.

Sophie didn't acknowledge his comment. Every now and then he slipped in statements that showed his feelings for her hadn't changed. Ignoring these comments seemed to be the best course. She woke up the screens and checked over the program coding displayed on the monitor. "This looks good. When the WITSEC mole accesses the info again, he'll pick up this tag and lead us right back to him." Sophie shivered in the room's air conditioning. The temperature was optimal for computers, not necessarily humans. Connor noticed, and handed her a sweatshirt. She slid her arms into too-big sleeves and wrapped it around her. "I want us to look into Hazel Matsue's supervisor, Deputy Supervisory Marshal Burt Felcher," she said. "Matsue told me that she did not log our secret location information. By going to see my father and his Secret Service agent at the Hilo Bay Hilton, I might have violated protocol. Once I did that, the Marshals Service could still claim their one hundred percent success rate, and if Felcher is the leak, he would not want to draw attention by violating that track record."

"This is just the information I needed. Now that I have a physical person to track, I can run down his activities, background, financials, etcetera." Connor settled in the chair beside her and cracked his knuckles. "Get ready to be hacked, Burt Felcher."

It was comfortable working alongside of Connor, surfing through data on the marshal collected from satellites, video cams, and surveillance equipment. They constructed a file on Felcher, tracking him at work, at home, even driving in his car.

"It is pleasant to be unfettered by any rules or concerns about the subject's rights or answering to a governing agency," Sophie said after some hours.

"Are you coming to the dark side?" Connor teased.

Sophie shook her head. "Only when strictly necessary, as in this instance. But I do see why you like this way of doing things."

In the days of investigation that followed as they applied themselves to the WITSEC case, Sophie felt herself gradually reengaging with the world and being able to maintain a cohesive focus. They exercised, worked in the office, then napped, or snorkeled, or beach walked. Sophie reveled in the mellow pace. She continued to gather all she could find on the Yām Khûmkạn, which didn't end up being anything new.

Pim Wat's stated goal of having Sophie develop online countermeasures made sense, given the organization's dinosaur online presence.

Connor and Sophie didn't have all they needed to trace the leak activity to Felcher, but the tracker tag attached to the Trojan spyware employed by the dirty agent eventually led him back to an IP address that could be physically checked out.

Connor knocked on the doorway of Sophie's room on her last day at his island retreat. "It's time to pass on this WITSEC case information we've gathered. Who do you think should get it?"

"It needs to go to both the head of the Marshals Service and to an outside agency to make sure that the leak is plugged," Sophie said. "We can keep an eye on the Trojan through the back door that you've created—but if the dirty agent finds our tracker, he can just install another RAT and we'll have to start all over again."

"I'll send the IP location and our data on to the head of the Marshals Service. From an anonymous source," Connor said.

"And I would like to send it to Freitan and Wong. They earned this, dealing with that body dump I found. They can provide some assurance that WITSEC acts on this."

Connor nodded and withdrew, leaving Sophie to her packing. Departure for Oahu and the trial had rolled around at last, and Sophie suppressed a feeling of dread as she packed her meager belongings— Mary Watson flirty skirts and feminine blouses that Connor had purchased. She could leave everything behind, but she was planning to spend the night at her father's apartment before the trial, and wouldn't have any clothing.

Sophie zipped up her duffel and picked up her computer bag. Ginger nudged her thigh, seeing the signs of departure.

"You seem like you have enjoyed your time here," Connor said as she joined him in the spacious entry room.

Connor had given her respite in his remote island getaway, and Sophie knew it. Her skin glowed with health and sunshine, her hair was a lustrous nimbus of curls, and she felt deeply rested in spite of the upcoming challenge of the trial.

"I have enjoyed my time here. It's paradise, truly." Sophie was uncomfortable with the intensity of his gaze. "I thank you for your hospitality. It has been a most welcome break for me to be somewhere completely safe."

"Consider this your home away from home."

"I do not think so." Sophie could not be anything but truthful. "But I'm grateful for all you've done for me." She couldn't look at him as she walked out, Ginger at her side.

Anubis and Nam the houseman were sad to say goodbye too, but soon Sophie and Ginger were settled on the Security Solutions jet flown by Thom.

Connor sat at his onboard workstation, dressed in immaculate business casual with freshly darkened hair, his eyes hidden behind colored contacts once more as he scrolled on a tablet.

Sophie opened her laptop and busied herself reviewing the notes she had made for her testimony in the Akane Chang case.

The notes were extensive. The district attorney had sent her a list of questions likely to be put to her by Chang's defense, and ones he wanted her to answer to set up the prosecution's case. Sophie built her testimony off her notes from the file of her and Jake's activities on their last case together. She felt a little pang of emotion every time she saw Jake's name, remembering the things they had been through together trying to find a missing young woman.

Jake had been there for her when she crashed from the emotional upset of her mother's reappearance into her life. He had shown depth of character that she had not thought him capable of. She missed him in an elemental way, longing for the heat of his body, the rumble of his voice, the sound of his heart against her cheek.

Each of the men in her life enriched her in such different ways. Her connection with Alika was comfortable friendship, spiritual and grounding, encompassing years of shared experience and physical compatibility. Her connection with Connor was stimulating, fascinating, a meeting of the mind, an adventure of titillating possibilities. And her tie to Jake was visceral. She even missed his smell.

She needed more time alone, unfettered, to figure out her own heart. Maybe when the Chang case was over, she could resume the explorations she'd been making through the Islands before her journey was derailed by Ginger's discovery of a murdered family.

Sophie got up from her seat now that the jet was leveling off and went to sit beside Connor in his sleek leather lounger. He was working on his tablet, his fingers flying.

"Is the Ghost looking for a new case?" Sophie asked as she sat down.

"You could have a look at what I'm working on anytime you care to open the program." Connor didn't look at her.

"Why are you so annoyed?" Sophie asked.

"Because you will not forgive me, and we've run out of time." Connor's mouth pinched tightly.

Sophie had not expected such an unvarnished, truthful statement. "I forgave you when you brought Ginger out to Thailand. I should have told you then." Sophie persevered when he still didn't look up. "I would like to be friends. Colleagues. To work together on the cases that we can, that intersect with shared agendas. I will collaborate with law enforcement and systems; you can do what you choose to do."

Connor looked up at last, his gaze anguished. "Do you think I want things to be like this?" He whispered harshly. "Don't you think I want to have a—more normal life? But I cannot have that because I must do what I must do."

"But why?" Sophie's query was a cry from the heart. "Why are you so compelled?"

"Because I can do what no one else can, I have a responsibility. To whom much is given, much is required."

"Even I have heard that saying." Sophie shook her head. "You are making a choice. Your statement is a belief. Dr. Wilson tells me every belief should be examined for its functionality. Who appointed you policeman, judge, and jury of all the evil in the world?" Sophie had never asked him how he'd become the Ghost, what process had brought him to this point.

But in this moment, she knew she was afraid to ask, afraid to know anything more, afraid that further disclosures would draw her deeper into his world and strengthen their connection...*she was in deep enough already.*

Connor blew out a sigh, leaning back to take his glasses off and rub the bridge of his nose. "I have been thinking about your skill set and your desire to work with law enforcement. I made no secret of the fact that I hoped you would join me in the mission of the Ghost. But since you have made it clear that is not something you'll do, I would like to propose an alternative: a special team."

Sophie stared at Connor as he stood up, moving back and forth in the central area of the jet with catlike grace. "I don't want you just to be an asset for the CIA. They do not have your best interests at heart —trust me on that. But we can use the opportunity of your mother's proposal that you join the Yām Khûmkạn as Security Solutions' first foray into counterintelligence. We can work for the CIA together, on our own terms. You can screen and investigate the Yām Khûmkạn on multiple levels, using the Security Solutions company and resources as a filter and a shield. *We* will decide what the CIA gets and doesn't get."

"How do you know the CIA does not have my best interests at heart?" Sophie stayed with something she could keep him talking about as she considered his proposal.

He paused to stare at her, his hands on his hips. "Really? You're asking me this?"

"Do they know about the Ghost?"

"Not that I'm aware of. Their cyber intelligence is not the best, and the Ghost works mostly online. But I've seen enough of their operations to know that when an asset's usefulness is ended, they dispose of him or her. I do not want that to happen to you."

"And you think you can protect me?"

"I know I can." Connor's voice rang with conviction.

He probably could. *But then she'd be dependent on him.*

Sophie covered her face, dropping her head into her hands. "I know I need to respond to my mother, and to the CIA. I've been dreading it." She dropped her hands and looked up at Connor as clarity lit her like a torch. "I want to work on the Big Island for now. Near Dr. Wilson, so I can strengthen my recovery under the guidance of a trusted professional. You've seen me. You know I'm not strong enough psychologically for such a role at the moment."

Connor's artificially dark brown eyes were opaque and unsettling. "Just don't do anything with the Yām Khûmkạn without talking to me first."

"Then perhaps we should call my mother now."

A long pause as Connor contemplated her. Finally, "I will give you a secure phone line through my computer that she cannot tap, and we will record the conversation. You can use Security Solutions as a shield even now."

Sophie narrowed her eyes. "You mean I can use *you* as a shield."

Connor tightened his lips and did not reply.

Once again, Sophie battled resentment that her mother had come into her life with nothing but a selfish motive. She had complicated Sophie's life even further at a time when Sophie was already strained by having an assassin on her trail, cases that haunted her, and relationship stress.

The depression hovered at the edges of her vision, flapping black wings at her, and Sophie remembered that she hadn't used Dr. Wilson's nasal spray in over a week.

Connor input the number that Sophie had been given by Security Solutions, and dialed.

Pim Wat answered, her voice smoky and familiar, speaking Thai.

"Mother, it's Sophie."

"Sophie Malee. It took you long enough to respond."

Connor reached over and squeezed Sophie's hand. His grip was strong, the support of someone who loved her. *Anti-venom against the poison of someone who did not.*

"Mother. I am in the middle of a very dangerous case, which I hope will be wrapping up soon."

"I am aware, and concerned. You must take precautions and stay safe."

"Almost sounds like you care." Sophie released a breath and let go of the sarcasm—it could hurt their negotiations. "I am thinking over your proposal, and I have questions."

"I do care. Ask your questions." Pim Wat was annoyed. "Not everyone is as emotional as you, Sophie Malee. Some of us show we care in other ways."

Sophie couldn't get into an argument with her mother about her utter lack of anything that had ever translated to Sophie as love. She switched to English so Connor could follow the conversation in real time. "What does the Yām Khûmkạn need me to do? I won't do anything illegal."

"There has been a penetration into our organization. Money is being siphoned off, and our agents' names have been posted to Interpol watch lists. We need you to find out who is manipulating us online and close the breaches."

"I do not need to be in your country to do that kind of work. You can grant me remote access to your databases. I can set up firewalls and protections for you remotely and pursue the creator of the breach online."

"There are those in our organization who do not trust you," Pim Wat said. "We want to have you physically present and our own tech agent checking your work."

"You mean, metaphorically or even literally, holding a gun to my head. And if your agents are good enough to check my work, they are good enough to do it themselves. So far you have offered me nothing of interest, Mother." Sophie glanced at Connor, and he nodded encouragingly. "What will the Yām Khûmkạn offer me for this work? And before you tell me money, I will tell you that I am not interested in that."

"Please, Malee. I have something you will want." Pim Wat's voice changed to soft pleading. Sophie remembered that tone from her youth: *"Fetch me a cup of tea, Malee. Rub my feet, Malee. Get in bed and hold me, Malee."*

Sophie suddenly remembered something she had not allowed herself to: there had been times, when her mother was deep in the depression, that Sophie had slept in bed with her, warming her mother's body with her own.

That reminded her of Jake and his unusual way of handling her own episode. Her eyes stung with tears. *The fruit hadn't fallen far from the tree...*

Her mother went on. "I will give you Assan Ang's criminal network. His contacts, his suppliers. Everything. Did you think that Assan did all his business alone? No. He was valuable to the Yām Khûmkạn because he had connections all the way into mainland China's heroin trade. We can give you all of that information now that he is gone."

Connor squeezed her hand, and Sophie saw warning in his eyes. *He knew something about this.* She needed to stall.

"Finally, you are telling me something that I might find interesting. But I would need a way to go after Assan's network for this to have any value."

"I'm sure you could interest Interpol or the CIA in this opportunity," Pim Wat said. "Assan had many enemies in law enforcement."

"I will consider this and get back to you," Sophie said.

"One week. No more. We have wasted enough time and have already begun looking for another hacker." Her mother ended the call abruptly, and the severing stole Sophie's breath.

Connor checked a small icon in the corner of his tablet. "She is in Hawaii."

"Or, she just wants you to think she is." Sophie got up and paced around the confines of the plane. "You of all people know it's easy to fool a trace."

"That aside. Did you consider my proposal? This is the perfect opportunity to take down one of the most entrenched, embedded crime organizations in Southeast Asia."

"Do you mean the Yām Khûmkạn? Or Assan's network?"

Connor's eyes crinkled at the corners. "Well. We'd begin with Assan's network. It's hard to tell exactly what the Yām Khûmkạn's modalities are from the outside, as we've discovered."

"Would we tell them we're working together?"

"The CIA, yes. They take you as a Security Solutions employee, or not at all. Pim Wat? The less that viper knows, the better."

Viper. Sophie still couldn't hear her mother described that way without a barb of pain, true though she knew it to be. "I just need to know that the Ghost has my back, as Marcella would say." Sophie faced Connor. "And that we'll work together to dismantle Assan's network."

"Of course. Coming soon: the complete disembowelment of Assan's organization, and the infiltration of the Yām Khûmkạn." Connor's eyes gleamed with excitement behind the screen of his glasses, and Sophie felt an answering spark.

For the first time, his contacts didn't bother her.

CHAPTER THIRTY-THREE

THE LIMO from the airport pulled up at Frank Smithson's swanky building in downtown Honolulu. Sophie had called her father to let him know she was arriving that morning and would be in her Mary Watson disguise. Dressed in a floral sundress, a concealing pair of sunglasses, and a large straw hat, Sophie felt as invisible as if she were wearing armor as the vehicle pulled up to the curb.

Connor reached across the seat and touched Sophie's knee. "I called the U.S. Marshals Service. Deputy Marshal Matsue, whom you worked with before, is on her way to meet you at your father's apartment."

"I'm sure that's not necessary. The trial is tomorrow, and this building has plenty of security."

"We don't want to take any chances." Connor said. "Not at this late date."

Sophie tightened her lips in irritation. "All right." She stepped out onto the sidewalk when Thom opened the door, giving Ginger's leash a tweak. The Lab jumped out of the limo to stand beside her on the sidewalk. "Goodbye, Connor. See you after the trial."

He waved briefly from the dim confines of the limo, his face a neutral mask, and Thom closed the door.

Sophie slipped Thom a wad of cash as she said goodbye. "Thank you, Thom. You are a wonderful pilot."

She walked up to the building's dignified entry and pushed open one of the smoked glass doors, her gaze taking in familiar elegant furnishings: marble floors, a crystal chandelier, and quality paintings in gold frames. She approached an elderly security guard behind a rounded desk at the back of the lobby. "Mary Watson to see Ambassador Smithson." She held up her ID.

"Yes, he called down to expect you—and you have a visitor." The guard pointed to a figure seated in a tapestry armchair, hidden in the shadow of one of the potted palms.

Sophie's heart jumped.

It was likely Matsue.

"Thank you." She walked across the room, her heeled sandals ringing on the marble—and pulled up short at the sight of the man seated in the chair. "Alika."

"Sophie." Alika slid something into his pocket and stood up. Ginger gave a happy yap and strained toward him. He patted the Lab's head. "I needed to see you."

Alika wasn't wearing his usual sleeveless Fight Club tee and workout shorts. Elegant black trousers and an open-necked silk shirt in a deep gold color emphasized his warm skin tone and amber eyes. Thick black hair waved back from his broad forehead, and his full, chiseled lips curved in a smile.

Sophie blinked at his magnificence. "I didn't expect you," she murmured. Her mouth felt numb. Her heart roared in her ears. The dream she'd had of the two of them flying over his home on Kaua`i flashed through her mind. "How did you find me?"

"Your father. I called him, told him I had to see you. He let me know you'd be here today." *Clearly, Alika was Frank's favorite of her suitors.*

"I'm in disguise. The trial." Sophie forced the words past the tightness of her throat.

"I guessed that. You look beautiful. What should I call you?"

Alika tilted his head. *That smile—so brilliant, so kind.* He accepted her secrets, always had.

"Mary. Mary Watson."

He took a step closer. "Hello, Mary. May I speak with you privately?"

Sophie flushed at the husky tone of his voice, the heat in his eyes. She looked around, abruptly remembering the threats she should be monitoring. "Not here. You can come up with me to my father's apartment."

The security guard caught her eye. "Before you go, Ms. Watson, you have a package."

Sophie frowned. "What kind of package?"

The guard took a medium-sized, flat rate postal box out from under the desk and set it on the counter. "Postmarked the Big Island. From a Dr. Wilson."

"Oh, Dr. Wilson." Sophie let out a breath. Dr. Wilson knew about her Mary Watson persona. *Maybe the psychologist had sent some more medication or some therapeutic reading material.* The guard lifted the barrier flap of his desk and walked toward her, carrying the box.

Ginger pricked her ears, leaving Alika's side, and trotted toward the guard. She hit the end of her leash and barked, a loud, inquiring sound. The hairs on Sophie's neck stood up, and she moved to stand in front of Alika. She slid her hand into her purse and curled her fingers around the cool pebbled grip of her Glock.

But Ginger seemed more interested in the package than the guard, sniffing at the box thoroughly. "Probably some cookies in here," the guard smiled.

Alika stepped around Sophie and took the box. "I'll carry that for the lady. Thanks."

Sophie watched the man, innocuous with his heavy bifocals and balding head, as he walked back to the desk. *Connor was probably right to have called the Marshals Service.* The security here definitely wasn't what it could be.

Alika had reached the elevator and pushed the button. The doors opened immediately, and he stepped inside, the package tucked under his arm. "Which floor?"

Sophie headed for the elevator, tugging at Ginger. The dog had decided to investigate the potted palm. "The penthouse."

Alika reached for the control panel as Sophie neared the doorway —*and the world exploded.*

CHAPTER THIRTY-FOUR

A LOUD RINGING.

Muffled thumps, tones, a wailing.

A red glow somewhere.

Ripples of throbbing sensation that made her grit her teeth.

PAIN.

The sounds sorted themselves into voices, somewhere overhead but far away.

Thoughts swam through her mind, random and disconnected, like sparks drifting from a bonfire.

Alika had come to see her. Ginger was misbehaving, as usual. *Her father was going to be upset that she was late.* Why would Dr. Wilson send a package without telling her? She should have refused it…

The light above Sophie became abruptly brighter. And then it was a lance, piercing her eye, delving into her brain. *Everything hurt.*

Consciousness burst upon her aching brain like an echo of the explosion. Sophie heard a pitiful noise, the dregs of a scream. She was making the noise, and it was tiny as a kitten's mew.

The box had been a bomb.

Alika had been holding the box.

179

Sophie screamed again. She heard the cry through the ringing of her ears, only slightly louder than before.

"You're okay. Just relax. Just breathe." An unfamiliar voice, very close. "You'll feel better soon. We're getting you some medication. Just breathe."

But breathing hurt most of all.

"Alika. Ginger." Sophie forced her mouth to form the words in spite of the pain, the heaviness on her chest, the thin gruel of air dribbling out between her lips.

"You will be fine. Just relax. You have some broken ribs, so breathing is going to hurt. But you are going to be okay."

She would never be okay if Ginger and Alika were gone.

More voices. People were moving around her, making puppet shadows against the red backdrop of her eyelids.

"Alika!" She whispered. Her throat burned.

A period of time went by, but Sophie was not present for it.

SOPHIE WOKE to a persistent beeping sound that accompanied the thumping of her head. She opened her eyes slowly, afraid of what she would see.

The surroundings were entirely unremarkable: putty-colored walls, a beige curtain on metal rings, the foot of a bed. Deputy Marshal Hazel Matsue, sitting in a chair across from her, was working on a laptop set on her knees.

Sophie was inclined at an upward slant. Her head ached. Her mouth was extremely dry, and every breath seemed to shred her lungs. She coughed.

"You're awake!" Matsue set her laptop aside and stood up hastily. She pressed a button near Sophie's hand.

Sophie's gaze slid down to that appendage.

An IV was taped to the back of it. Her skin was lacerated, and there was a bruise on her arm. A plastic bracelet circled her wrist. *Mary Watson* was printed in blue on the plastic band.

"Thirsty." Sophie's voice was a rasp.

Matsue picked up a plastic cup and held a straw to Sophie's lips. "They said you could drink all you wanted. Your internal organs are fine."

Sophie drank. With each sip she drew energy back into the battered husk of her body.

She wiggled her toes. Her legs seemed intact. She moved her arms. A burning, rubbing sensation told her that she had skin damage. But it was when she tried to draw a deeper breath that she felt the most serious pain, a stabbing weight to the chest. Her eyes widened as panic swelled, increasing the sensation.

Matsue touched her arm. "Your doctor is being paged. He will tell you what happened. But you are all right."

"Alika? Ginger?" Sophie's voice was still a thread.

Matsue tightened her lips and shook her head. "Wait for the doctor."

"Where is my father?" *Her dad would be so worried...*

"You are in protective custody. No one can visit you right now. I'm sorry, Sophie. Until the trial is over, you are completely sequestered."

Sophie tried to draw breath to speak, her heart galloping, but it was too difficult. Her head swam. She shut her eyes.

"Ms. Watson."

Sophie opened her eyes to see a man in a white coat in the doorway, a uniformed marshal behind him. The doctor, a diminutive Asian with large spectacles shielding mild eyes smiled as he approached her. "I'm Dr. Heng. I see you're awake, Ms. Watson. Just relax. Let me give you something for the pain." His voice was gentle as he injected something into the IV.

The glasses reminded her of the man in the lobby. "The security guard. The package," Sophie whispered.

"Yes. You were the victim of a bomb." The doctor picked up

Sophie's wrist, feeling her pulse. "I'm going to check your pupils. They were unevenly dilating before, indicating some swelling to your brain from the impact of the explosion. You were thrown backwards ten feet or so, and you landed hard."

"My dog?"

Matsue spoke up from her position near the chair in the corner where she stood while the doctor performed his examination. "Ginger is fine. In fact, she is the reason you have broken ribs. She landed on you when you went down."

"Yes. Other than a concussion, dermal lacerations, and bruising, you have three broken ribs. I would say you were a very lucky young lady."

"And Alika?"

"Your friend was not so lucky." The doctor's voice was matter of fact as he continued to handle her body as if she were a doll.

Sophie felt nothing for a moment. Then grief hit, a boulder falling on her from a great height.

"No." Tears rose in a wave to burst out of her eyes. "No, no, no!" She needed to get away, to crawl to somewhere dark where this unbearable feeling couldn't crush her. Pain knifed through her chest as she hyperventilated. She thrashed at the doctor, at the IV, and tried to rise from the bed.

Hands held her down. Voices were a storm overhead. Then, merciful oblivion.

CHAPTER THIRTY-FIVE

SOPHIE WOKE FEELING TOO HOT.

She cracked her eyes open. The room was dark; but she didn't hear hospital sounds any longer.

That's right. They'd discharged her.

Matsue and her team had spirited Sophie out of the hospital, heavily drugged and disguised, in a wheelchair. She was in the downtown Honolulu safe house condo where they were keeping her, heavily guarded, until her testimony the next day.

Sophie shut her eyes. There was no reason to open them. *There was no point to anything.*

She would do what was expected; Matsue had told her she was going to be called as a witness tomorrow, if the trial proceeded as projected. But why bother waking up? Sleep was an escape from a truth too terrible to bear.

Still, she was too hot and something heavy weighed her down. She shoved at it, whimpering at the twinge of pain from her ribs.

"Hey. You're awake." Jake's voice in her ear. *He was lying in bed with her, close against her side, and the weight was his arm across her.* "Am I hurting you?"

"Jake," Sophie whispered. "You came." Her eyes overflowed with easy tears.

"I knew you were in Witness Protection, but I was freaking out—especially after the bomb went off in your dad's building. No one would verify whether or not you were involved." Jake paused the rush of words, snuggling her close. His bulk was a furnace of warmth. His lips brushed her neck. She inhaled his delicious smell, and her muscles went slack. She closed her eyes, inhaling comfort.

He went on. "Matsue got in touch with me yesterday; she had called Marcella, who said you needed a trusted friend. They let me come to help guard you."

"Alika…" Her throat closed.

"Poor guy. The dude almost died. I knew you had to have been there when I heard a woman was also injured, though they wouldn't release any names."

"He's alive?" Sophie turned in Jake's arms, groaning at the pain from her ribs, at the expansion of hope stretching her battered emotions.

"Yeah. Mangled, but alive." Jake sounded surprised. The room was too dim for her to see his expression.

"I thought he had died." Sophie closed her eyes and exhaled a long slow breath. "The doctor said he wasn't so lucky…"

"And he wasn't. Dude's still on life support."

"Oh no." Sophie ducked her head and pressed her face against Jake's chest. She choked on a sob. "All my fault."

They could never be together. She was as deadly to Alika as one of her mother's poisons. But at least he was alive; he might someday recover. Guilt swamped her. Jake murmured soothing noises and rubbed her back as she wept. Eventually she slept, enfolded in his warmth.

SOPHIE HELD up her hand and looked into the bailiff's eyes. The woman was a well-rounded mixed-race female of indeterminate age, packed tightly into a navy-blue uniform. Her dark brown gaze was compassionate. "Do you solemnly swear to tell the truth, the whole truth, and nothing but the truth, so help you God?"

"I do."

"You may take the stand."

Sophie turned and walked with the aid of a cane up into the witness stand of the small, drab courtroom. She was subject to random waves of dizziness, and short of breath due to her ribs, but nothing would stop her from testifying at this point—she'd have crawled into the courtroom if necessary—and the DA had told her that the bruises, lacerations, and obvious signs of injury added to their cause.

Due to the nature of the case, the courtroom was closed to spectators. Sophie was relieved that she didn't have to face a wider audience as she scanned the room. Akane Chang's hate-filled eyes burning holes in her were more than enough hostile scrutiny. The defendant, wearing a classy gray suit, sat in the front row with his lawyer, a muscular blonde wearing chunky statement jewelry.

The prosecuting attorney walked over. "Let's begin by having you tell us about your role in a Security Solutions investigation into the disappearance of a young woman on the Big Island."

Sophie looked across the courtroom to where Jake was seated behind the prosecution's table. Their eyes met. He gave an encouraging nod—*his testimony would back hers up, just as he always backed her up.*

Sophie took a deep breath, blew it out, and plunged into the dark tale that had led to this moment.

CHAPTER THIRTY-SIX

BYRON HAD BRIBED Akane's lawyer to wear a button cam during the trial. He was able to have a front row seat to watch the pile of evidence against his brother, assembled by the investigative team of detectives and the district attorney, unfold. He watched a battered Sophie Ang testify, making the vital missing connection between his brother and the multitude of bodies found in the ditch on a road outside of Volcanoes National Park.

Byron endured hours of watching Akane's lawyer try to chip away at Ang and her partner's credibility, at the way the investigation had been conducted, always emphasizing the lack of physical evidence. She seemed to be making some headway until Julie Weathersby, the fresh-faced young woman the Security Solutions team had been seeking, took the stand to testify to Akane's threats and rape attempt at knifepoint.

Byron watched the jury's faces as Julie, trembling with fright, told a harrowing tale and exhibited a pink scar just below her jawline, where Akane had held her at the edge of his blade before her escape.

His brother wasn't going anywhere.

Byron heaved a sigh of relief and wasn't surprised when the

adjudicators didn't take long to deliberate and soon came back with a guilty verdict. Akane was sentenced to multiple life, and bound over to be transported to a federal prison that specialized in security for well-connected criminals.

The lawyer tried to calm Byron's raging brother as Akane spewed threats on the occupants of the courtroom.

"Terence was right. You're a rabid dog, Akane, and you need to be put down," Byron murmured. He pushed a button and turned off the cam's feed playing on his laptop.

He sat back in his office chair, laced his fingers over his belly, and contemplated a beam of light falling through one of the high windows of his historic warehouse office. His security team was on alert outside the building, Lani was outside his office keeping order, and his brother was safely and forever behind bars.

Byron had navigated this particular minefield and come out on the other side.

No one in their organization would fault him for trying to kill Sophie Ang, the woman whose testimony had brought Akane down. He even had a ready answer for whomever had threatened him for doing so: *he'd tried to call off the Lizard.* The man had refused to take his call, listen to his messages—and the Lizard was clearly incompetent, because he hadn't finished the job, either.

It was five o'clock somewhere, and he deserved a celebratory drink. Maybe Lani could come in and drink with him. They could do it on his desk after.

Byron got up and poured each of them a generous tot of well-aged whiskey from the bottle he kept in a cabinet behind his desk. He depressed the old-fashioned intercom on his desk. "Lani? Get in here."

"The computer repairman has arrived, sir." Her voice was professional. "I'll be just a moment."

Oh yeah—she'd complained about getting some kind of virus on her machine. He returned to his desk and sat down, sipping his whiskey.

He heard a sort of muffled thump through the closed door and frowned, his hand dropping to the weapon he kept handy on his desk. Not that he was jumpy, or anything—it was just good to take precautions. He depressed the intercom again. "Lani?"

His door was already opening.

The Lizard stood there innocuous and deadly, dressed in a computer repair coverall.

Byron glimpsed the gleam of light on metal and lifted his weapon —but the assassin in the doorway fired two first.

Byron recoiled against a bloom of pain in his chest, an unspeakable heaviness. His hand came up to touch the area. He looked at wet, shiny, bloodstained fingers in disbelief.

Everything was going spotty: black, white, red. He couldn't breathe.

The door opened wider.

Behind the Lizard's back, Byron could see the body of his lover sprawled across her desk.

"I paid you." Byron's voice was a thread of sound.

"But you tried to call off the job. I'll take your life as forfeit, and consider this black mark on my record expunged."

The black bore of the Lizard's silenced pistol opened up and swallowed Byron whole.

CHAPTER THIRTY-SEVEN

THE LAST PERSON Alika expected to see when he opened aching eyes was his grandmother Esther Ka`awai.

Tutu was seated beside his bed, crocheting. Sunlight, filtered through a light-diffusing blind in the hospital window, fell softly over long black hair threaded with silver and braided over one shoulder of her *muumuu*. Tutu's weathered brown hands moved quickly, confidently over the soft pink yarn, working on a small bowl shape. *She was making a baby hat.* Her mouth moved—she was praying.

He was in a hospital bed. *Again.*

And whatever had happened had been bad.

"Tutu." Alika's voice was a rusty whisper he hardly recognized.

"Oh, my grandson!" Esther set aside her crocheting. "Finally, you're awake!" She picked up a Styrofoam cup with a straw and held it out, pressing the plastic tube to his lips. "They took you off all the machines yesterday."

Alika sucked the entire cup of water through the straw, and when he spoke, his voice was stronger. "That box was a bomb, wasn't it?" He was surprised to feel so mentally alert—he could remember everything about the moments leading up to the explosion.

"Yes. It's a miracle you lived. God has a plan for you, *mo'opuna*."

Alika's lips were sore as his mouth moved in an ironic smile. "Some plan." *Someone else had been with him during that explosion.* "Sophie? How is she?"

"I don't know why you're asking about her—didn't you two break up? The woman and her dog who were with you in the lobby were injured, but okay." Tutu picked up her crocheting and resumed. "The police say it was a random hate bomb. Thank God it wasn't bigger. They think it was supposed to go off when you were in the elevator with the door closed."

Alika shut his eyes, exhausted by the small effort of drinking the water. *Sophie was okay.*

Pain was a dull throb off in the distance, held at bay by medication. But things felt different in his body.

"You'll learn to deal with this, I know you will," Tutu's voice. "People live with this kine thing plenty and it never holds them back."

"What kine thing?" Alarm prickled along his nerves. Alika opened his eyes again and struggled to sit up. Tutu pressed a button and the back of his bed lifted up slowly.

He looked down and surveyed himself. "What the hell?"

His brain took minutes to process that his left arm was gone, because he could still feel it. Feel everything about it, even a sense of the damage it had taken, a burning pain around and above the elbow. He tried to lift the arm, could swear it even moved—but there was nothing to see but a bandaged stump at his side, resting on the blank white of the hospital sheets.

His grandmother's eyes were shiny with tears. "You will be okay, *mo'opuna*. You don't need two arms to be a whole man."

Alika couldn't take it in. His head swam. He shut his eyes and focused on breathing.

ALIKA'S FIGHT CLUB manager Chewy was the next visitor he woke up to. "Hey man. You're looking good." Chewy's beard was characteristically thick around his toothy grin. Thick, tatted, ropy arms rested on his knees. He held a small item in big ham hands.

"I expect that line of crap from my grandma, but not from my business partner." Alika's eyes felt gritty, and there was something nasty he didn't want to remember. *Oh yeah.* He'd lost his arm. "God bless it."

Somehow his *tutu* was wearing off on him in his old age. No swear word felt big enough to encompass how thoroughly the universe had screwed him over. Multiple times now.

"You're alive, which is a lot more than most people would be in your shoes. I was there; I got to see how bad it was."

Alika stared at his friend. "What?"

"You probably don't remember, but you made me your emergency contact here on Oahu. I got called by the emergency personnel. Got to the building in time to see them load what was left of you on a gurney and haul you away." Chewy shuddered. "I thought you were gone. Never seen so much blood in my life."

Sophie. "What about the woman who was there with me?"

"She was unconscious and pretty worked over, but they told me she'd likely be fine. Her dog did the most damage; guess that Lab flew backwards into her and smashed her ribs. But the dog got up and was running around. They had a helluva time catching it."

Ginger must have been frantic, terrified. Alika shut his eyes, replaying the scene, wishing he didn't have to.

Chewy went on. "The cops interviewed me. Wanted to know what you might have been doing at that building. All I could think of was that it was Sophie's building, right? You must have been going to see her." Chewy held out the object he'd been holding—a small black box. He popped it open. "You had your good shirt on. And this was in your pocket."

Alika's gaze focused on the band of brilliant, channel-set diamonds in platinum resting on a bed of black velvet.

Memories bubbled up sluggishly.

He'd been in touch with Frank ever since he got to Oahu after his one night with Sophie, and he'd taken the man into his confidence. He'd told Frank he wanted to ask her to marry him, planned to offer her a different kind of life. More settled, but still her own. He had no problem with any of the shit Sophie was into as long as she took reasonable precautions and came home to him. He'd told Frank his vision of them living on Kaua`i, running a gym together, her traveling to do her investigation work, maybe a couple of kids someday.

He still remembered Frank's face, beaming with happiness as the ambassador shook his hand. "If I could say 'yes' for my daughter, I would. That's just the kind of future I want for my girl." The man had clapped him on the back that fateful morning and sent him down to wait for Sophie in the lobby.

Alika's chest spasmed with grief. He shut his eyes to hide his emotion.

He had nothing to offer Sophie now—and he knew how her mind worked. She'd disappeared on him before, sure she was dangerous to him. Now, she'd be so sick with guilt she'd never want to see him again—*because there was no doubt he'd been holding a bomb that was meant for her.*

"Hey, man." Chewy's voice was rough. "I'll just hold onto this ring for you. I'll put it in the office safe. In the meantime, don't give up. I'm keeping your friends and family from swamping this room right now. Your parents are on their way—they just went down to the cafeteria for a few. You're gonna come back from this better than ever. You've done it before. You're like the freakin' Terminator, man. I think you should get a bionic hook for that arm."

Alika opened his eyes with an effort and made himself smile. *He had come back before; this was worse, but Tutu was right. His life had been spared for a reason.*

But that reason didn't involve Sophie. He was done with this particular struggle.

"Thanks, Chewy. Keep the ring. Give it to someone special. I won't be needing it."

CHAPTER THIRTY-EIGHT

Pɪᴍ Wᴀᴛ sᴀᴛ on a bench at Ala Moana Park on Oahu. The ocean sparkled in the late afternoon sun. A tiny tropical breeze teased the leaves of a huge, spreading banyan tree overhead. Children played on equipment not far away. A smooth arc of yellow sand before her was cluttered with tourists, the busy sounds of the city behind them lost in the music of little waves.

Pim Wat tossed bread crumbs to a host of pigeons, hopping and pecking around her feet. Filthy creatures—she hated them. But in her current elderly woman disguise, they were just right to help play out her Script.

She liked the way her hands looked, their youthful smoothness hidden by cheap net gloves with the fingers cut off. Baggy, food-stained garments completely obscured her beautiful body, and Pim Wat smiled, just a little. She was so good at this. *Too bad no one celebrated her secret triumphs but faithful Armita.*

She slid her left hand into one capacious pocket, curling her fingers around the state-of-the-art Maxim 9 pistol with built-in suppressor, a gun she'd bought at the prototype stage because she liked the futuristic look of its matte black, boxy shape and the utility of its design—she always needed a silencer on her weapons. *Might as well get one that was small and efficient.*

Pim Wat checked the angle of her shot—as long as the man she was meeting sat on her right, she'd be able to fire right through her skirt from the left, and he'd never know what hit him.

The assassin known as the Lizard was supposed to be meeting her here after a long, careful series of communications she'd initiated through his website. She had baited the Lizard to this meeting by telling him she knew he was behind the murder of Byron Chang and his top people, information she'd received by text from her unknown informant.

The Lizard was good with a sniper rifle, so Pim Wat wore sweat-inducing body armor under her oversized garments. She couldn't wait to get this meeting over with, and to strip everything off. She already had a massage scheduled for this afternoon.

An elderly man shuffled toward her, carrying a paper bag that looked like it held breadcrumbs. She cursed inwardly, glancing sideways beneath the brim of her sun hat to assess the intruder as he sat down beside her.

The man's back was curved with age. He wore a pair of camouflage pants and a Primo Beer tee that had seen better days. A canvas fishing hat, trimmed with dangling lures, shaded a liver-spotted brown face mostly obscured by thick trifocals. "You like feeding the pigeons, too?" His voice was raspy and hopeful.

Pim Wat ignored him—*she had to get this fool to leave.* The last thing she needed right now was some misguided old man trying to scrape an acquaintance.

"They are just feathered rats, but useful for cover," her companion said.

Pim Wat's heart jumped so hard she almost gave herself away with a startled movement. *The Lizard was right beside her!*

Fortunately, she was still holding the pistol at the ready. She raised it slightly. The cold metal rested on her thigh, pointed toward him.

Pim Wat had expected someone much younger, possibly even a woman, and no doubt disguised. But this man's face and hands were wrinkled and spotted in a way that could not be faked. His movements had been perfect!

Rage filled her. *She'd almost been duped!*

The Lizard set the bag of breadcrumbs on his knees. "You asked for this meeting."

She didn't want to talk to him. She didn't want to negotiate. She just wanted him dead, this man who had tried to murder her daughter.

Pim Wat shot him.

The Maxim 9 made a noise like a balloon popping, louder than movies portrayed. The pigeons flew up, a maelstrom of flapping wings.

The Lizard recoiled, hit in the midsection. He pulled his hand out of the bag of breadcrumbs to reveal a silenced Beretta, and shot Pim Wat.

The impact, square in her chest, knocked her backward and stole her breath. She clutched the bench's support with her right hand and pulled the Maxim out of her pocket with her left.

The Lizard was down on the bench beside her, gasping for air just as she was. No blood showed—he was wearing a vest, too.

She'd worry about breathing later.

Pim Wat hauled herself upright so she was looking down at the Lizard, and shot him in the face.

The outcome wasn't pretty.

His body went slack on the bench, and he slid down to lie flat on his back. His hand dropped, the Beretta falling to the dirt. The paper bag, still on his lap, tipped over, spilling bread crumbs over the ground. The pigeons descended again, a fluttering, macabre horde.

Pim Wat glanced around—no one was looking in their direction. She could still hardly draw breath but managed a few tiny sips of air as she staggered dizzily around the body to retrieve the fisherman's hat where it had fallen off of the assassin's head.

She dropped the hat over the Lizard's ruined face and retrieved the Beretta, slipping it into her other pocket. Standing beside him, she emptied her bag of crumbs. The pigeons swarmed around them. A child waved and laughed in their direction from the beach.

The stage was set—an old man, feeding the pigeons, had fallen asleep on a park bench.

Her Script was complete.

CHAPTER THIRTY-NINE

SOPHIE RESTED her head on her father's shoulder, sinking deep into his hug. She'd just come all the way up the stairs to his penthouse, unwilling to ride the elevator, and she and Ginger were both exhausted from the effort. "So glad the trial's over," Frank said. "You've given me some serious gray hair these last couple of months."

"I'm sorry." The apology seemed to encompass a vastness of things. "We did it. Akane Chang's going away, and Marcella told me the Chang operation is in disarray." Sophie had hardly been processed out of the Witness Protection Program and said goodbye to Hazel Matsue, when Marcella had called to let her know that Byron Chang had been shot in his office, along with his secretary and a couple of bodyguards. "I think it's safe for me to return to the Big Island."

Her father held her away to look into her face. "You're kidding me, right? Nothing good ever happens to you there. You need to stay right here, in my apartment, and recover. Maybe start going to that gym of Alika's again when you feel up to it."

"I won't be seeing Alika anymore. He almost died because of me." Sophie turned away from her father to look out of his apartment's floor-to-ceiling windows, breathing past the pain in her chest. She'd missed that iconic view: Diamond Head's rugged extinct volcano outline, the gleam of light on skyscrapers, surfers on the inside, a squall blowing in, trailing a rainbow way out to sea.

"Alika wouldn't want you to take it that way," her father said softly.

Sophie frowned at him. "The man lost an arm because of me. We're done." Jake had told her the final extent of Alika's injuries, and she could hardly stand to think of it. "Don't bring him up again, Dad."

"Coward." Her father's mouth tightened as he fisted his hands on his hips. "You owe him at least a goodbye."

"None of this is any of your business." Sophie's temper flared. "Why did you tell him I'd be coming to your place the day before the trial? If Alika hadn't met me in the lobby, he would be a whole man right now. I had already decided that my lifestyle is too dangerous for a civilian. I told him that in Hilo and left him without any contact info. And you mucked it up, Dad, by telling him where to find me."

"And you'd be dead if he hadn't been holding that package." Her father's gaze was unyielding. "Alika loves you, Sophie. He can offer you a different kind of life. I want that for you, and I am never going to apologize for doing what I think is in your best interest as a parent."

"You don't get to make those kinds of judgments, any more than my mother does." Sophie's lips felt stiff as she forced the words out. Her body felt frozen, a pillar of ice. "I will choose my partner, my path, and my lifestyle."

"You are throwing your life away fighting dangerous criminals, and someday, you won't be the winner. You're my only daughter. *I don't want to stand over your grave!*" Frank's booming voice filled the room. His eyes filled and his hands balled into fists. "You are being selfish and foolhardy! At least consider going back to the FBI, to your tech lab! You didn't get shot at there!"

Sophie's heart raced in shock at Frank's raised voice—she couldn't remember a time her father had shouted at her.

Ginger yelped in distress. Sophie tugged Ginger's leash, striding away from Frank and into her bedroom. She closed the door and locked it. She sat down at her computers, blindly seeking some form of comfort in her old technological friends.

Sophie stared at the blank, dark monitors, feeling nothing but despair.

She'd changed—those "friends" that she'd named Ying, Jinjai, and Amara—they were just machines. They had no wisdom, love or even escape to offer.

She could count on one hand the number of times her father had lost his temper with her, and his words shook her.

In many ways, Frank was right. Her life had been one terrifying episode after another since she left the FBI—but it had never been easy there either, the depression whispered. *You're cursed, and someday you'll kill your father too. Give him a heart attack or a stroke from the stress of being your parent.*

Her dad could never know how close she'd come to killing herself. She'd have done a much more effective job of causing him grief than any outside enemy could have.

And Alika did deserve at least a visit, but she knew she wouldn't go. She *was* a coward—because she couldn't stand to see his pain and loss. *Suffering she'd caused.*

Sophie's body hunched in misery; she tugged her hair so that the pain without matched the pain within.

She struggled to remember Dr. Wilson's words from one of their therapy sessions. "The depression has its own voice. Don't believe everything you think."

"Foul demon depression, filling my ears with lies," she muttered aloud. *"Demented sickness of the mind, I reject you."*

A soft knock at the door. "Sophie. I'm sorry I yelled."

Sophie got up and opened the door. "Dad. I'm sorry, too."

Her father embraced her, but she felt unable even to lift her arms and hug him back; she was trapped and paralyzed inside her own body.

Her father sighed. "I don't understand you, Sophie. Just like I never understood your mother."

Her dad didn't know the half of what Pim Wat was, and hopefully he never would.

More guilt stabbed Sophie. "I'm definitely going to the Big Island. I was just getting started on some things over there. Personal things." She needed to get to Dr. Wilson and talk through all of these events, get back on her medication, have another infusion. *Something!*

Her father made a snorting noise and addressed the dog. "Hear that, Ginger? She's going to take you away again for more camping adventures."

The Lab woofed in reply. Sophie bent to reach down and rub Ginger's silky ears. "She understands everything you say, Dad. And no, I'm done camping for the moment."

"How was Witness Protection? Where did they keep you stashed all that time?" He was trying to move them past the fight, but every topic was fraught.

"I can't tell you, Dad." *How could she explain the weeks on Connor's private island?*

Frank led her into the kitchen. "Want something to eat? Marcella brought over a ton of food from her parents' restaurant."

"I could eat." Sophie found herself using a Jake-ism.

Jake.

Jake would make her feel better. She was a little addicted to the comfort and warmth of his arms. Nothing got her to relax quite like his hugs.

She was weak, and battered, with a sickness of the mind barely in remission. Jake made her feel better, and he loved her. If he could accept her exactly as she was, maybe that was enough for both of them.

CHAPTER FORTY

Sᴏᴘʜɪᴇ ɢᴏᴛ out of her father's Lincoln on the tarmac of the private aircraft area of the Honolulu Airport, and he exited the vehicle, too. Ellie Smith, who had driven them to the airport, popped the trunk for Sophie's bag.

She'd ended up spending three days at her father's apartment, resting her ribs and recovering: sleeping in with Ginger, visiting Marcella, and letting her father buy her a new wardrobe: movement-friendly pants, plain, well-cut, richly colored button-down shirts, a panoply of silk underthings, and a handbag made in Morocco of antique tapestry fabric that was big enough for her laptop.

"Thanks for everything, Dad. I really needed those restful days with you." Sophie hugged her father goodbye. "You were right about a lot of things you said the other day. I'm sorry I've been a disappointment."

"No, Sophie. Never that. But I worry." Frank clasped her close, careful not to touch her tender ribs. "Please be careful of yourself." He kissed her forehead.

"I will." She kissed his cheek. "Bye, Dad."

Ellie picked up Sophie's heavy backpack to spare her injury.

They headed for the Security Solutions jet, its door ajar and stairs to the runway already extended.

"What did you decide about the Yām Khûmkạn?" Ellie slowed their walk toward the jet.

"I'm going to work with the CIA on that. But with backup," Sophie said.

"What does that mean?"

Sophie opened her mouth to answer, but Jake appeared in the doorway of the jet. Sunshine gleamed on his hair and the muscles revealed by a sleeveless workout shirt. He bounded down the steps toward them with his usual energy. "Aloha, Agent Smith. Let me get that bag." Jake swung the heavy backpack out of Ellie's hand and onto his shoulder like it weighed nothing.

"When did you two meet?" Sophie frowned, trying to assimilate the surprise of seeing Jake appear out of the plane.

"Jake brought Tank to your dad's place to play with Ginger several times before your pup was whisked away to join you wherever you were hiding before the trial," Ellie said. "Speak of the devil." She pointed.

The black-and-white pit bull, looking much sturdier than when they'd first rescued him, stood in the doorway of the jet. The dog's huge mouth was open in a grin and his stump of a tail wagged so hard his hind end seemed to be doing a hula. Ginger gave a happy yap and lunged forward, yanking her leash out of Sophie's hand. She scrambled up the stairs to greet her friend.

"Match made in heaven," Jake grinned.

Sophie dodged eye contact and looked back toward Ellie as Jake loped ahead with her bag. "Thanks for your help. With everything."

"Your father counts on your phone calls. Please keep in close touch, or I'll have to send the Secret Service after you." Ellie chuckled, but Sophie knew she meant it.

"Fair enough." Sophie waved goodbye toward her father's car and focused on climbing the steps of the jet. Breathing still hurt, and she held a hand over her ribs. Her ribs were strapped, but it was more to remind her not to make any sudden movements than for any thera-peutic benefits to be had from the stretchy Velcro wrap.

"Ribs are the worst." Jake glanced at her from where he was stowing her backpack in an overhead compartment. "They hurt like a mofo and there's not much anyone can do to help the healing process."

"So it seems." Sophie looked around the plane. "Where's...Mr. Hamilton?" *She'd almost slipped up and called him Connor.*

"Hamilton's on one of his mysterious business trips." Jake secured the dogs by their leashes to a convenient handle and settled them in a pair of plushy beds.

"Okay, now for the obvious." Sophie put her hands on her hips. "What, exactly, are *you* doing here?"

"The boss man has asked me to help you set up a new Security Solutions satellite office in Hilo." Jake looked up, a shadow in his gray eyes for the first time. "You're on board with that, right? Hamilton said it was your idea."

Was this how Connor was going to handle her request to stay on the Big Island? It appeared so. "I'm eager to discuss the plan with him."

They were interrupted by the appearance of Thom Tang and his copilot, emerging from the cockpit. "Good to see you again, Ms. Ang. Just a little hop this time."

"Thanks, Thom."

They exchanged pleasantries. "Sit down, get comfortable, and enjoy the ride." Thom and the copilot disappeared.

Jake's brows rose. "You seem to be on good terms. What was this about 'just a short hop this time'?"

More secrets to keep from Jake, who hated them. He was like a bloodhound on a scent when he sensed subterfuge. "Thom brought me from the Big Island into Witness Protection custody."

"That's the same hop we're about to take," Jake pressed. "He acts like he knows you, like he's flown you further than this."

Sophie folded her lips together and settled herself into her seat.

She fastened the belt and gazed out the window as Jake sat down beside her.

She felt his nearness draw her in like a force field. *That much hadn't changed.*

"I missed you," he whispered. "Even a few days away is too long."

The time Jake had spent with her, recovering from the blast in the Witness Protection safehouse, had been platonic but very physical. She'd slept in his arms and awoken to his hugs. She'd missed his warmth, his sheer bodily presence.

Sophie shut her eyes, savoring the contact as Jake drew her into his arms. He leaned into her and kissed her, his body hot against hers. The G-forces of the jet's takeoff pressed them deeper into each other.

Sophie was sad, hurting, filled with guilt and regret, and apprehensive about what would come next on the Big Island and with the Yām Khûmkạn. *Jake made her feel better.* He lifted her burdens as easily as he lifted her backpack. No, she didn't love him the same way she loved Alika, but she loved him as much as she could—*and maybe he loved her enough for both of them.*

Sophie turned fully toward Jake, turning over in the comfortable lounger to face him. She met his gaze, enjoying the honest heat of his eyes. His brows raised in question.

"Jacob Sean Overstreet Dunn. Would you...be my lover?" Her voice quavered.

"Sophie. What you do to me." He cupped her cheek with a big hand and stroked the scar on her face with his thumb. He wiggled his brows. "You had me at Jacob."

She laughed a little and covered her face, flushing with embarrassment and vulnerability.

Jake pulled her hands away and held them. "What changed?"

"I almost died. And I want to feel alive." She couldn't say it any more clearly. "You make me feel alive."

The mist gray of his irises were circled in blue, like a rainy day with the promise of sunshine. "Just so we're clear—you're agreeing to my terms. We're together. Exclusive."

"I am, exclusively, a wreck. You have been warned. But if you still want to take your chances…" Her eyes stung, and she closed them.

His answer was to kiss her. *Oh, what a kiss.*

His mouth seemed to breathe life into her. They kissed all the way to the Big Island, and the flight wasn't long enough.

CHAPTER FORTY-ONE

Pɪᴍ Wᴀᴛ sᴀᴛ quietly in a corner in the dimly lit, swanky Honua Club in downtown Honolulu. She'd arrived early for the meet to make sure she had a seating advantage; the hostess had put her in a corner booth facing the door at her request. The light from a window behind her would fall into the eyes of the man who sat in the seat across from her, and movement out of the booth would be hampered by deep leather upholstery.

She had played up her exotic looks with a designer wrap dress in a deep plum that made the most of her golden skin tone and petite, shapely figure. A fat diamond dangled in her cleavage, a handy focal point. Her long, smooth black hair tumbled down her back and swirled around her hips. A tiny designer hat with a swatch of veil perched on her head and hid her eyes.

She slid her compact out and checked her lipstick. *She didn't appear any older than her daughter.* She had years of pampered living away from the sun to thank for that.

Her gaze darted around the room, checking for threats, for anyone who might be surveilling her—but the restaurant's noontime bustle seemed normal, sound patterns controlled as servers whisked to and fro. The patrons, mostly men, conferred over micro-brews and top shelf liquor. Occasionally, bursts of deep-toned laughter leavened the air.

She sipped tonic water over ice with an olive, a drink with every appearance of alcohol, but contained none.

Her lunch date appeared at last, weaving between the tables confidently. *He knew this place.* This was his turf, and she'd chosen the Club for that reason. He drew up short at the sight of her, though, and his eyes widened.

Pim Wat smiled, enjoying her effect on him, and tipped her head back just a little so he could see her eyes behind the veil. She'd lured him to the meeting by using her daughter's Mary Watson alias, a bit of intel she'd received via text from her anonymous source a while back. She extended a beringed hand to the older man. "Supervisory Marshal Felcher. Thank you for making the time to meet with me."

"Ms. Watson. A pleasure." Felcher was almost stammering. The marshal had well-kept hands, and he held hers a moment too long. "I am eager to hear this information you have." He swung his trim body to sit beside her on her side of the booth.

She removed her hand as his proximity forced her to slide around the booth toward the back. She cursed inwardly—*he'd boxed her in, and now the sun was in both of their eyes.* "I had to speak to you."

Felcher gestured for the server. "Perhaps we could have something to drink. Coffee, please. Black."

Pim Wat had studied his habits, and even with her visual cue of an apparently alcoholic drink, he was staying true to form. Her gaze fell to his coffee mug, upended on a paper doily. "I prefer something cold on a hot tropical day."

"To each his own. You have an intriguing accent, Ms. Watson. Where did you say you were from?"

"I didn't." She smiled.

The server poured Felcher's coffee, and he sipped. She sipped. They regarded each other.

"You asked for this meeting, *Mary.*" He used the first name deliberately, implying he thought it was false.

"I have information about a breach in the Witness Protection Program." Pim Wat wrapped her plump, scarlet lips around the minuscule straw that had come with her drink and sucked. She knew how it looked. She'd practiced it in the mirror.

Felcher watched her, eyes gleaming. "That is a very serious allegation. Very concerning. Perhaps we should go somewhere more private to discuss it?"

"I don't think so, sir. I hardly know you." She tipped her head regretfully.

"Call me Burt." He wriggled closer.

She slid further away. "Burt. Such an assertive name."

"I really think we should go upstairs. I have a suite here at the Honua Club that I use for private meetings."

"How prepared you are, Burt. Let's work up to that." Pim Wat put her hand on his thigh and squeezed. He stiffened in surprise, and she ducked her head so he wouldn't see her smile.

The waiter arrived with menus. Felcher waved him off, his gaze on Pim Wat's face. "How did you come by the name Mary Watson? You are not who I expected."

"No?" Pim Wat gazed up at him innocently through the mesh of the veil. "It is a common enough name. Whom did you expect?"

"Someone...taller."

Sophie Malee was indeed tall, at five-foot-nine. She got her height from her father. Pim Wat's cheeks went hot at the thought of the harm this man had tried to do to her child.

She sipped her drink. He sipped his coffee. Their eyes never left each other's faces.

And then it happened.

His eyes bulged. His mouth opened. His right hand flew up to clutch the left side of his chest. He turned toward her, panic and comprehension in his gaze.

"Paralysis of the heart muscle. Relax. Don't fight it; it will all be over soon," Pim Wat whispered, holding his terrified gaze. She scooted close and reached out to draw him against her. His body tensed, shuddered. His back arched. His eyes rolled back. She pressed his head into her neck in a hug that looked passionate to anyone passing by.

Her eyes tracked the room. No one was watching the tableau in the corner booth.

She held Felcher until he slumped bonelessly, and then she pushed him back upright against the booth's upholstery.

Felcher's face was turned toward her. His eyes were wide in a fixed stare, his color blanched. Pim Wat passed a hand quickly over his bloodshot orbs and closed them. She leaned in and dabbed spittle from his lips with her napkin. "There. You look perfectly rested, dear Burt. You should not have sold my daughter's information to an assassin. She is special, and I need her."

Pim Wat swiped the napkin over the table, over the upholstery, over everywhere she'd laid a hand or touched him, most especially around the rim of the coffee cup. The toxin was odorless, tasteless, and undetectable in the body—but it did leave a residue if not removed.

Her eyes moved constantly as she kept her body language natural, appearing to converse with a partner who couldn't take his eyes off her.

And then, when every back was turned, every server busy and guest occupied, Pim Wat slid out of the booth, tucked the napkin into her little purse, and walked out of the restaurant.

CHAPTER FORTY-TWO

Sophie looked around the small but well-appointed space in downtown Hilo, the site of the new Security Solutions extension office. A Security Solutions SUV had met them at the airport and whisked them here. She was still a little in shock at how quickly things had been set up for their new location.

A picture window in the meeting area of their office suite framed a view of ruffled ocean, swaying palms, and the busy traffic that fronted downtown Hilo. Sophie liked the ambiance of the historic building with its high ceilings and shining dark wood floors.

Sophie had her own small office, and Jake another beside it. A third room, unoccupied, contained storage and file cabinets at the moment. The reception area was currently empty.

"This will do very well, Mr. Hamilton." Sophie turned to face Connor, who'd been waiting in the SUV that met them at the airport. "Very kind of you to take time from your busy schedule to facilitate opening our new satellite location."

"Anything to make sure my best operatives have all they need." Connor leaned against the empty receptionist desk, his arms crossed on his chest. "I've put a temp agency on retainer. They can provide you with clerical support. Just give them a call when you're ready."

Jake emerged from the empty room in back where he'd been poking around. "We do need someone to answer phones, handle intake and manage our schedules and billing. Unless Oahu has enough work to keep us busy and can keep piping us cases..."

"Bix will funnel cases this way as they come through the Oahu office." Connor hadn't taken his dark eyes in those hipster glasses off Sophie. "But you two are responsible for generating enough new work on the Big Island to justify this extension." He straightened away from the desk. "I'll leave you to it. Sophie, a word before I go?"

"Of course." Sophie followed Connor as he went into her work space and shut the door. He turned on a handy fan. The whir provided white noise as he stalked toward her. He removed his glasses and set them on the desk.

"There's been activity on the WITSEC leak."

Sophie's brows drew together. "You got a report from the Marshals Service? They're moving on our tipoff?"

"No. Felcher's dead. Heart attack. Appears to be natural causes."

Sophie covered her mouth with a hand. "That's awfully...convenient."

"Isn't it?" Connor took a step closer. She didn't feel his anger until he was standing so close they were almost touching. "You were making out with Jake on the plane."

"Yes. He's agreed to be my lover." Sophie stared into Connor's eyes, hidden by those contacts. "He makes me feel better."

"You should be with me." His voice was harsh. He gripped her arms. "I want you to be with me."

"What you want is irrelevant." She broke his grip, whipping her arms up out of his hands, stepping back. "You had your chance, Connor, and you broke my heart."

"You said you forgave me." He was still angry. Now she was, too.

"I did forgive you. I'm here, working with you, aren't I? But that doesn't mean I have feelings for you anymore."

Connor spun away. Paced. Cursed in Mandarin. "Do you love Jake? If you love him, I'll leave this alone."

"I don't know. I just know I need him right now."

They were both breathing hard. She couldn't help noticing their breathing had fallen into sync. He cursed again. "I hate this. I thought we were...getting somewhere, finally."

"You did this to us, Connor. You."

"I want to fix it. How can I fix it?" He whirled away, shoving a hand through his darkened locks.

"You can't fix it. It is what it is." She thought of Alika's broken body, of his missing arm. Tears welled up. "None of us is getting what he or she wants." She covered her mouth with a hand.

Connor stopped, looked at her. "Alika. That's who you love."

Sophie turned to look out the window. "He's paid too high a price to be with me. I won't see him again. Ever."

"And Jake is..."

"Jake is necessary."

"That sounds like love."

"Maybe. I don't know. I just know I need him."

They looked at each other a long moment.

"All right then." Connor squared his shoulders, rolled them back. "If you need him, then you need him. I love you enough to want you to have whatever you need, even if it's someone else. That's what love is, Sophie."

"I'm sorry," Sophie groaned. "This hurts."

"We won't discuss this situation again—but let me know if it changes, will you? Because I want you, and always will." Connor's eyes could still see her soul, even with those contacts on. "We'll meet soon, to discuss liaising with the CIA and a plan to penetrate the Yām Khûmkạn." He blew out a breath. "I won't be watching you anymore. You have Jake to protect you now."

He walked out and shut the door a little harder than necessary.

"I don't need anyone to protect me," Sophie muttered. She

wrapped her arms tightly around herself and stared out at the view. Her broken ribs ached.

Just keep breathing. Breathe, breathe, breathe. *It will get better someday.*

Jake opened the door. "What was that about? Hamilton seemed pissed off."

"It's nothing. We're meeting tomorrow." Sophie didn't turn.

Jake came up behind her. He wrapped his arms around her shoulders and pulled her stiff body close, tucking her head in beside his chin. His warmth surrounded her, his strength supported her. Gradually Sophie relaxed, sinking into him with a little sigh, closing her eyes, letting go.

"Want to break in this desk properly?" His voice was a sexy rumble beside her ear.

She laughed. *No one made her laugh like Jake did.* And in the war against her inner darkness, laughter was a sword.

Turn the page for a sneak peek of, *Wired Fear*, Paradise Crime Thrillers book 8.

SNEAK PEEK

Day One

Seated on the top step of his front porch, Terence Chang surveyed the fenced yard of the Chang family's former compound as his two brindled pit bulls wandered and sniffed around. He was proud of how neat the place looked now: he'd removed the many junked cars, the rusting freezer, and the pile of barrels his cousins had stored meth-making chemicals in.

Terence sipped his coffee. He liked it black, and fresh, made from one hundred percent Kona beans grown on his own plantation, one of his several legitimate businesses. He sipped again, letting the fragrant brew roll around on his tongue, settle on his palate. He looked down at the expensive black basketball shoes that were one of his few indulgences.

He had made many good changes. *He had tried hard to go straight.* He'd built up his own legit business online, and run interference for the family via computers, and until now, that had been enough.

But his cousin Byron, acting head of the family, had been gunned down recently, along with his receptionist and bodyguards. It hadn't been long since the brutal slaying, but the Chang family empire already seemed to be coming apart at the seams.

Worst of all, Terence's psycho cousin Akane Chang had somehow escaped jail on Oahu before he could be transferred to a maximum-security prison in the Midwest to begin serving multiple life sentences.

There were those in the family who thought Akane should take over in the vacuum left by Byron's death, that Akane's brutality and bloodthirstiness were signs of strength.

Terence knew better.

He sipped his coffee, trying to regain the simple pleasure it had given him only moments ago.

She had liked his coffee, too.

He refused to let her name arise in his mind—but it did anyway. *Julie Weathersby.* His own personal kryptonite.

Julie's face filled his mind: wide blue eyes, happy smile, those pale freckles on her nose. The little sounds she made in his arms. The way she snuggled into him, trusting as a puppy.

He'd never been anyone's hero before.

Terence tightened his mouth bitterly. The coffee suddenly tasted like ash.

He'd rescued Julie—picked her up on a deserted road wearing nothing but her underwear, running for her life from Akane. He'd prevented that brutal rapist batshit crazy serial killer cousin of his from tearing her apart, emotionally and physically.

What he hadn't counted on was falling for the girl.

Letting himself hope he could have some other kind of life and share it with someone special.

But he couldn't have her. Or that life. Because the worst thing that could happen to the Changs, and everyone around them, would be for Akane to take over the business.

Akane had friends who owed him. Side hustles no one knew anything about. And if Terence didn't step up to take Byron's place, there was a very good chance Akane would come out of left field, waste anyone who offered competition, and bring on a reign of blood like the Changs hadn't been through since the thirties, when they'd warred with the Chinese triads for power and come out on top.

The phone rang on the step aside him, and his dogs looked up, pricking their ears. Terence read the ID window: *Hilo PD*. "Terence Chang here."

Nowhere to hide. No point in trying.

"This is Detective Freitan from Hilo PD. Your cousin Byron Chang's crime scene has been released. Your name was on the deed of the warehouse building where he was murdered, hence the call. I suggest you contact a cleaning service that specializes in biohazard cleanup and blood removal before you go back to the premises."

Freitan was a badass mofo of a female detective. Terence's balls crawled for cover whenever he had the misfortune of dealing with her. "Thanks for the call, Detective. What can you tell me about efforts to capture my deranged murderer cousin?" *No sense glossing over the truth.*

"Not my case, Mr. Chang. His capture is an FBI matter. I'm sure someone will be in touch with you soon to find out possible locations where your dear family member might hide." Freitan sounded hard, flippant.

Terence took another sip of coffee to wet his throat. "I appreciate any support Hilo PD can give me in capturing Akane. Believe me when I tell you, we don't want him around here."

"I heard you were going straight, Terence. But you sound like you're speaking for the family on this matter." Freitan's tone was serious.

"I'm speaking for the family, yes," Terence said. It was time to 'shit or get off the pot,' as his beloved but terrifying *tutu*, Healani, had always said, and it couldn't hurt to establish his authority with the local PD early on.

"Your concern about Akane's capture is noted," Freitan replied. "I'll let the FBI know that you are their official point of contact."

"You do that." Terence ended the call with a punch of his thumb.

He had a lot of arrangements to make, starting with getting in cleaners to remove all trace of the carnage of Byron's murder. He needed to get the downtown warehouse space ready for a big meeting, and there was no time to waste.

Terence went back into the house, already working his phone. The dogs trailed him in.

He wasn't going to get the girl or the life he'd hoped for, but he would get the office that had been Byron's, and his father's, and his grandfather's—and maybe, just maybe, he could eventually steer the Chang empire in a different direction.

First, he had to step up and take the reins, and even that wasn't going to be easy.

The dancers whirled across the stage in perfect unison, the stomp and slide of bare feet on the stage emphasized by a hypnotic Hawaiian chant and the thump of an *ipu* gourd. Fern headdresses gave a feeling of royalty to the dancers, as did the swirling capes of long, lustrous black hair whirling around their hips. Full skirts, covered with an additional layer of ti leaf, both concealed and enhanced every crisp, defined movement as the dancers told a story through their bodies. Even security specialist Sophie Ang, unfamiliar with hula, could feel *mana*, supernatural power, vibrating through the performance.

As the action came to a crescendo and ended with the dancers' arms raised high and heads bowed, Sophie's eyes prickled at the power and pathos. Even watching on the small screen of the phone the client held was mesmerizing; she couldn't imagine how intense it would be to witness such a spectacle up close, in person. "Thank you for showing me that. It really helps me to understand why the Merrie Monarch Festival is such an important cultural event here in Hilo," Sophie said.

A mixed Hawaiian/Asian female who looked approximately thirty years old, the client, wore the kind of fitted floral-print muumuu that indicated a service industry job. A name tag over her left breast spelled out KIM KAUWA. Sophie whisked a price tag off one of a pair of chairs in front of her desk, new since they'd opened the Security Solutions extension office a week ago. "Please, come sit down. Can we get you something to drink?"

"No. In fact I can't stay long." Kim's eyes darted nervously to the door, where Sophie's partner Jake Dunn lounged, arms crossed on his chest.

"Jake, come in and join us. Let's all get comfortable. Tell us how we can serve you." Sophie liked to think she was getting better at the social niceties, though it was a mental effort to grapple with the mechanics of engaging others after so many years behind a computer.

Kim took a seat, her purse clutched close. "I looked up your business online. The website said you had a brand-new location here on the Big Island, and I just…wondered if you might be able to help me. Us."

"That's what we're here for. Helping people." Jake extended a hand and Kim shook it briefly. Seated, he was still an intimidating sight, his muscular torso packed into a black polo-style Security Solutions logo shirt that left no doubt that he spent a good deal of his free time at the gym.

Jake made small talk with Kim while Sophie scanned the intake form the woman had filled out in the lobby with their receptionist, Felicia.

Kim was thirty-eight years old, lived in Hilo, and worked for the Hawaii Tourism Authority Board as well as Hawaiian Airlines customer service. She was a volunteer organizer for the famous annual Merrie Monarch Hula Festival that was taking place soon in Hilo. Under "Needs that bring you to us" Kim had listed, *"confidential concerns regarding the Merrie Monarch Festival."*

Sophie looked up and met the woman's dark brown eyes squarely. "Before you get into telling us about the situation that brings you here, and I gather it's sensitive from the way you filled out the form, let me assure you that this initial consultation is completely confidential. We will not disclose anything about your work with our agency to anyone. But perhaps you should know a little bit more about what we do so that you can make an informed decision."

Sophie described the various programs that Security Solutions offered, from the patented artificial intelligence "nanny cam" software installed at high security locations to more typical security and alarm monitoring. Bodyguarding, kidnap rescue, and private investigator services were also available wherein she, Jake, or both, served as private detectives working on behalf of the client or a lawyer.

"That's what I need. Private investigation." Kim knotted her fingers together over her purse. "I'm representing the Hawaii Tourism Authority in this situation. We give a big grant to the Festival every year. I'm also one of the organizers. Well, it seems some of the Festival's money is missing."

Sophie exchanged a glance with Jake. Any investigation that could be done online, such as tracking a money trail, was a strength for Sophie. "Tell us more."

"It's all very sensitive. The event is so culturally important that… well, even asking questions about something like where the money went…I could get plenty *pilikia*." Kim slipped into pidgin, the Hawaiian creole dialect Sophie was becoming familiar with.

"Don't know *pilikia*, but I get the feeling it's not good," Jake said. "Are you sure you don't want to go to the police with your concern?"

"Oh no. No!" Kim recoiled. "Everybody is related to everybody else on this island and has connections—word would get out we're looking into it for sure if I went to the Hilo PD, and we just aren't ready with anything concrete." She took a deep breath, calming herself with an obvious effort. "Let me begin at the beginning. The reason I chose Security Solutions was that you're new in town, and no offense, but you're *haoles*." She looked Sophie up and down, clearly taking her golden-brown skin into consideration. "Outsiders.

That's what *haole* means, and that's what I need. A confidential team, with no local networks, to dig into where the money's going."

"How much money are we talking about?" Jake leaned forward, brows knit over steely gray eyes.

"A hundred grand. That's just the Hawaii Tourist Advisory board money. There might be more that's missing, I don't know. The Merrie Monarch competition is supported by a lot of bigger businesses such as Hawaiian Airlines. I work for them, too, and liaise with their charity office to facilitate support of the Festival." Kim coughed a little, hiding her mouth with a hand. "Maybe I need something to drink, after all."

Jake stood up with his usual restless, coiled energy, clearly needing to move. "Let me get you some tea. Sophie, anything?"

"Hot tea would be fine. Thank you."

Jake disappeared. Through the office door, Sophie heard the rumble of his voice bantering as he spoke with Felicia at her desk.

She met Kim's eyes. "I don't know much about the Merrie Monarch Festival. I will have to research it. As you may have noticed, it's only been a week since we officially opened our doors. But we have all the resources of our parent company on Oahu behind us. Would you like to know a little about my background?" Kim nodded, and Sophie went on. "I'm a former tech agent with the FBI. I can find most anything online. I love tracking money trails." She cracked her knuckles and rippled her fingers as if using an imaginary keyboard.

This seemed to help put Kim at ease, because the woman smiled. "You both seem...impressive." Her gaze tracked over Sophie's body, dressed in the simple black polo shirt and nylon combat pants that she and Jake had decided would be their "uniform" unless they were undercover. "Like you two work out a lot."

"We do. Part of the job. We need to be prepared for any sort of emergency. Jake's ex-Special Forces with much investigative experience. And you are right in your assessment. We are outsiders here in

Hilo. I'm glad that, for once, it's a strength." Sophie shrugged. "We enjoy using our skills to help people."

"You have an accent. Where are you from?" Kim raised her brows curiously.

"I'm American and Thai. I grew up in Thailand and was educated in Europe. I only came to live in the U.S. five years ago."

Jake returned with Felicia in his wake. The pretty blond grad student from the University of Hawaii carried a tray with tea makings on it. She had been sent over from the temp agency Security Solutions had contracted with to help get the agency's satellite office going, and so far, Sophie found her personable and smart.

Felicia set the tray, with its mismatched collection of mugs, on the edge of Sophie's desk. "Anything else I can get you?" Her gaze was fixed on Jake in mute adoration.

Sophie felt a twinge of something unpleasant tighten her gut. Felicia must not know she and Jake were involved. Sophie bogged down mentally trying to figure out how to tell her; she'd have to just kiss Jake in front of the girl or something. "Thanks, Felicia, that will be all."

The receptionist left, shutting the door behind her, and Jake dealt with the tea until all of them had what they wanted. Sophie wrapped her fingers around her hot mug as the beverage steeped, warming her hands. "Kim. Please continue. When and how did you begin to suspect something was wrong?"

"I helped facilitate the grant to the Festival. I'm not on the Festival Board, so I don't have access to the financial reports. But it seemed to me the same sponsors were being featured, and the budget is available to organizers to view, and it's roughly the same. Only this year, PR and advertising wasn't nearly at the same level as in the past. Everywhere I turned at the planning meetings I was hearing that we didn't have the money, but I knew the Tourism Board had given the same amount, and like I said, the overall budget was similar to last year's."

Jake frowned. "So you don't have anything more tangible than that?"

Kim looked down at her hands in her lap. "That's why we can't go to the police yet. And when I say 'we' I'm talking about me and my *kumu hula*, Esther Ka`awai."

Sophie jerked, feeling as if she'd been zapped with a red-hot wire. Esther, a well-known Hawaiian wise woman, was Alika Wolcott's grandmother; and Alika was a painful subject to be avoided at all costs. "Isn't Mrs. Ka`awai on Kaua`i?"

"I am studying under her. Esther provides cultural advisory oversight to the event. She was the one to put the pattern together and really bring it to my attention. She is able to do a lot long distance." Kim was apparently oblivious to Sophie's discomfort. "She and I decided to try to get more information without tipping anyone off that we were looking into it."

Sophie squelched her apprehension at the thought of interacting with Esther Ka`awai. "So which of you is the client?" Sophie looked down at the application in front of her. "And to put it bluntly—who will be paying the bill?"

"The Tourism Advisory Board will be hiring you. I went to them with our concerns, and they gave us a budget." Kim named a figure. "Can you work with that?"

"We certainly can," Jake said. "And to start, we will need all the names and contact numbers that you can give us for everyone involved with the Festival."

"I have that on computer. I'll email it to you."

"We need to get eyes on the different players and areas involved," Jake went on. "Do you have a plausible way to introduce us, bring us around to meetings and such?"

"Something closest to the truth is always the best," Sophie said. "Jake tends to stand out as a cop or investigator no matter what. Bringing him around as a private security expert to help make sure nothing's stolen or unsafe makes sense. My skills lie behind a computer. I'll be looking for the money trail from the bank. Let's come up with a plan and timetable on how to proceed."

"I'd like us to get started right away," Kim said. "The Festival is in a month, and the sooner we find out where the money went, the sooner we can get it back and put it to work to make this the best event ever." Her brown eyes shone almost feverishly. "We owe it to our people."

Continuing reading *Wired Fear*: tobyneal.net/WFweb

ACKNOWLEDGMENTS

Aloha dear readers!

Thanks so much for whirling through another roller coaster of a book with me! *Wired Secret* really wrapped up the events that were begun in *Wired Justice*, and opened a whole new chapter for Sophie going forward, working with Jake on the Big Island and delving deeper into the situation with the Yām Khûmkạn that will continue, along with a juicy new case, in *Wired Fear* #8.

You don't know how close Alika came to being killed in this book. Actually, he *was* killed, in my first version of the scene. That night, I was too upset to sleep. I've had so much difficulty figuring out who Sophie should be with! I also remembered that, five years in the future of Paradise Crime's timeline in *Bitter Feast*, Lei Crime Series #12, Alika's still alive.

So, I resurrected him, and by the time this series ends, he's going to be a veritable saint with all the trials he's been through: a sort of Zen Terminator. I love that guy, in spite of how he keeps getting the short end of the stick! Don't count him out yet, he's not done being a part of this adventure—in fact, he might still be its destination.

This book was Sophie's "dark night of the soul," even more than *Wired Dark* was. I truly didn't see her almost suicide attempt coming

—that scene sprang straight out of the black heart of her depression, and I'm frankly sorry we had to go there. In writing a character that suffers from clinical level Major Depression, I'm taking you on a journey into that disorder as Sophie learns to manage and overcome this "sickness of the spirit" in all its debilitation. The ketamine treatment Dr. Wilson gives her is a very real intervention that shows a lot of anecdotal promise and is currently being used rather widely through private clinics. Most of the treatments are given as infusions, because the dosage is more easily controlled and effects can be better titrated. But nasal sprays are also used, and I thought that would work better with the plot. If you or someone you know is suffering from treatment-resistant depression, ketamine is a possible intervention to try. Just search 'ketamine treatment for depression' in your area, and you might be surprised by what you find.

A quick caveat: in the opening scene, Hazel Matsue and Kamani Freitan both are armed. In a "real" situation, they would likely have surrendered their weapons upon entering the jail. In most states, only the corrections officers are allowed to carry firearms. But this is a work of fiction, after all, and sometimes the story reads better with a few embellishments.

I thought it was past time that I mention why I'm interested in Thailand (besides that it's a beautiful paradise of a country with lovely people and a gorgeous rich culture.) For many years, my husband and I have supported dear friends who founded a Christian orphanage, Baan Santisuk (Home of Peace and Happiness) in Phang Nga, Thailand. We have never visited Thailand, but over the years have come to be interested in its food, culture, and people due to this connection. My mental health background has even come in handy a few times in advising how to support some of the more traumatized orphans. Visiting our friends Mark and Dorien at the orphanage someday is at the top of our travel bucket list! In creating Sophie, a half-Thai character who adores children, I've found a way to enter that world a little bit.

I'm excited to announce that audiobook recording has begun on the Paradise Crime Series with the very talented Sonja Field (who did Unsound and my romances.) Her sexy foreign-influenced British accent interpretation of Sophie's voice is so wonderful! I can't wait for you to have yet more ways to enjoy these books.

Every book "takes a village" to be born, and once again I'm thankful for my support team: my awesome business manager, Jamie Davis, a new "tech consultant" reader, Walt, and my faithful copyeditors, Bonnie and Don, along with Angie my wonderful Typo Hunter. Mahalo!

Thanks also to my dear fans in the Friends Who Like Toby Neal Books group; your help with my questions and concerns, participation in polls, and your positive response to snippets from the book kept me coming back to the page with energy and passion.

If you enjoyed *Wired Secret*, please leave a review! They mean so much to me, and to others looking for a good read. Your opinion, even in just a few words, matters more than you know.

Until next time, I'll be writing!

Much aloha,

FREE BOOKS

Join my mystery and romance lists and receive free, full-length, award-winning ebooks of *Torch Ginger & Somewhere on St. Thomas* as welcome gifts: tobyneal.net/TNNews

TOBY'S BOOKSHELF

PARADISE CRIME SERIES

Paradise Crime Mysteries
Blood Orchids
Torch Ginger
Black Jasmine
Broken Ferns
Twisted Vine
Shattered Palms
Dark Lava
Fire Beach
Rip Tides
Bone Hook
Red Rain
Bitter Feast
Razor Rocks
Wrong Turn
Shark Cove
Coming 2021

Paradise Crime Mysteries Novella
Clipped Wings

Paradise Crime Mystery
Special Agent Marcella Scott
Stolen in Paradise

Paradise Crime Suspense Mysteries
Unsound

Paradise Crime Thrillers
Wired In

Wired Rogue

Wired Hard

Wired Dark

Wired Dawn

Wired Justice

Wired Secret

Wired Fear

Wired Courage

Wired Truth

Wired Ghost

Wired Strong

Wired Revenge

Coming 2021

ROMANCES
Toby Jane

The Somewhere Series
Somewhere on St. Thomas

Somewhere in the City

Somewhere in California

The Somewhere Series
Secret Billionaire Romance
Somewhere in Wine Country
Somewhere in Montana
Date TBA
Somewhere in San Francisco
Date TBA

A Second Chance Hawaii Romance
Somewhere on Maui

Co-Authored Romance Thrillers
The Scorch Series
Scorch Road
Cinder Road
Smoke Road
Burnt Road
Flame Road
Smolder Road

YOUNG ADULT

Standalone
Island Fire

NONFICTION
TW Neal

Memoir
Freckled
Open Road

ABOUT THE AUTHOR

Kirkus Reviews calls Neal's writing, *"persistently riveting. Masterly."*

Award-winning, USA Today bestselling social worker turned author Toby Neal grew up on the island of Kaua`i in Hawaii. Neal is a mental health therapist, a career that has informed the depth and complexity of the characters in her stories. Neal's mysteries and thrillers explore the crimes and issues of Hawaii from the bottom of the ocean to the top of volcanoes. Fans call her stories, *"Immersive, addicting, and the next best thing to being there."*

Neal also pens romance, romantic thrillers, and writes memoir/non-fiction under TW Neal.

Visit tobyneal.net for more ways to stay in touch!
or
Join my Facebook readers group, *Friends Who Like Toby Neal Books,* for special giveaways and perks.

Made in the USA
Las Vegas, NV
19 January 2023

65868722R00142